She couldn't stand the

Julie breathed in ... e door and raced dow... d Matt, she threw he... fierce hug. "Well?" she whispered.

"Well, how about letting me get inside to sit down, Beautiful?" he said lightly. If it were good news, he would have spilled it the second he saw her. But his tone was too deliberate, too controlled. She felt sick with fear as she followed him to the living room.

Her eyes were fixed on Matt as he took off his jacket, draped it over the arm of the sofa, and sat down. He held out his hand. She took it, letting him pull her down next to him. Matt squeezed her hand tightly as she settled into the cushion. He looked at her. Deep-set gaze. Serious gaze. Julie needed to know, but suddenly she wanted to stop his words.

"It's Hodgkin's disease," he said quietly.

Julie's feelings were suspended on a current of shock. "Hodgkin's?" she heard herself repeat dully.

"Cancer," Matt said, without displaying any emotion himself.

Don't miss the other books
in this romantic series, **First Comes Love:**

To Have and to Hold

For Better, For Worse

Till Death Do Us Part

Jennifer Baker

SCHOLASTIC INC.
New York Toronto London Auckland Sydney

ISBN 0-590-46315-2

Produced by Daniel Weiss Associates, Inc.
33 West 17th Street, New York, NY 10011

12 11 10 9 8 7 6 5 4 3 2 1 3 4 5 6 7 8/9

Printed in the U.S.A. 01

First Scholastic printing, July 1993

One

"I'll make you a deal," Julie said.

Matt gave a contented smile. "After a meal like that, your wish is my command." He pushed his chair back from the dinner table and patted his stomach.

"The way to a man's heart, huh?" Julie joked. "Yeah, I know. You've stuck with me all this time because you knew that sooner or later I'd learn to cook."

"Right. Chicken parmigiana, lemon string beans, apple pie, and now you're the perfect wife," Matt said with a wink.

Julie rolled her eyes, laughing as she balled up her napkin and threw it at Matt. Matt exploded in a fit of coughing. Julie's laughter melted into a frown. "About that deal. I'll do the dishes if you get right into bed and take care of yourself for once," she said. "No getting up for anything until you have to go to work tomorrow. Okay?"

Matt nodded as his coughing subsided. "Thanks, Jules," he said hoarsely. "I'll cook and wash this weekend." He came around the table and leaned down to kiss the curve of her neck. Julie paused, dishes in her hands, and savored the feel of Matt's full lips, soft on her skin, and his familiar scent. She let her eyes close, giving over a moment to the pure pleasure of having Matt so near.

His kiss turned into a raw cough. Julie's eyes flew open. "To bed!" she ordered him. His winter flu was taking much too long to go away. "Didn't the doctor tell you to get plenty of rest?"

"Okay, okay," Matt said, backing toward the bedroom. "And, Jules? I do think you're the perfect wife. Really."

Julie smiled as Matt disappeared into the other room. *Wife.* She was actually starting to get used to that word. She stacked the dishes in the sink. At first it had seemed like a game, as if she and Matt were little kids playing grown up, playing house. But their little apartment over the thrift shop on Main Street, in Madison, Ohio, was finally beginning to feel like home—their home. And the incredible feeling of being loved so much—and loving so much—was strengthened by knowing that whatever lay ahead was something she and Matt would share.

Julie laughed softly as she filled the sink with warm, soapy water. Why did she deserve to be so happy over a sink full of dirty dishes? She'd never expected this when she'd started college this past fall. No way. Back then, with her good-bye to Matt still fresh and painful, she'd thought it was going to be four years of loneliness, four years of phone calls that could never substitute for being with him. And then had come Matt's surprise visit and the passionate night that had followed.

That whole weekend had felt like a dream: waking up in her dorm room in Matt's arms, racing to the Maryland border on his motorcycle, the wedding ceremony in the sunny, perfect, little town hall. And before Julie even had time to believe it was real, she was a married woman.

As she rinsed a plate and put it in the drainboard, Julie heard Matt washing up in the bathroom. It felt so natural now, sharing the rhythms of the day. But in the beginning, it hadn't been so easy. The first heady weeks of wondrous embraces had finally given way to a whopping dose of reality. Matt had given up his whole life in Philadelphia—his job, his friends, the mountains and lakes he loved. And Julie was pulled between college and Matt. The scariest part had been knowing that whatever it was they'd done, they'd done it for keeps. *For all the years of our lives . . .*

Had they made a mistake? They'd both wondered—silently at first, then their fears finally erupting into the kind of fights they'd never had before. Julie's face grew warm as she thought about how the tension had driven her into Nicholas Stone's arms. She still couldn't erase the memory of Nick's kisses, the way his lips felt meeting hers, the gentleness of his touch.

Julie sighed as she scrubbed a pot. Thank goodness for her and Matt that it hadn't gone any further. Still, her friendship with Nick hadn't been the same since, and now, two months later, Matt would barely even say hello to him. Matt's first friend in Madison, Ohio, and they weren't even on speaking terms. Because of her.

Julie tried to push aside all the uncomfortable memories. She and Matt had gotten past that. They were more in love every day. That was what was most important. Christmas vacation had been like a stay-at-home honeymoon—ice-skating at the quarry, cozy afternoons watching old movies on TV, a ride out to Lake Erie and a bracing winter hike along its sandy shore.

Now second semester was getting under way, and the second half of her year-long journalism course with Professor Copeland was looking better than it had last semester. Maybe, Julie thought, chuckling to herself, that was because she'd gotten over the worst thing about Copeland—meeting the guy and getting to know him. The A-minus he'd given for her first semester's work had been a bit of a shock. Not that Julie hadn't worked hard enough for it, but Copeland was a notorious scrooge when it came to handing out good grades.

"Hey, Jules?" Matt said as he emerged from the bathroom. He gave a little cough.

Julie half turned from the sink. "Yeah?" Matt came toward her, his thick, dark hair damp, a towel wrapped around his waist, his lean, muscular torso bare.

"What do you think about getting Leon to warm up the Cow Girls?" His words were punctuated by more coughing, but his deep-set gray eyes sparkled with excitement.

Four days a week, Matt worked as a waiter, dishwasher, and busboy at the Barn and Grill, the most popular restaurant in town. But every Friday night his bosses, Jake and Patricia Howard, let him throw the biggest, best party in Ohio, with live music and lots of dancing. The Barn and Grill had tripled their Friday-night business since Matt had started Club Night, and Julie hadn't seen him so psyched since he'd been running the Fast Lane, his father's club in Philadelphia. Plus, Jake and Pat had cut him in on the Club Night profits, which meant that once in a while there was even a little money left over after Matt and Julie paid their bills. A brunch out, a new CD—it meant a lot after struggling to get by all through the fall and early winter.

"I think it would be a hot double bill," Matt was saying. "Leon played me a couple of his new songs the last time I went over to his place, and they're awesome."

"Cool!" Julie said. "Put some homegrown talent onstage." Leon, known around town as "the Lip," was a friend of Matt's who could often be heard practicing his sax out on the town green in nice weather, or going over an imaginary riff in his head at the Black Angus Coffee Shop.

"I'm going to call him right now, see if he's into it," Matt said. The end of his sentence was swallowed up by another bout of coughing.

Julie put a hand on his arm. "No way, José. We made a deal, remember? You can call him tomorrow. Right now, you're getting into bed."

"Well, okay. I guess it can wait till the morning. But I'm only going to bed if you come with me," Matt said, putting a warm hand on her cheek.

"Matt—you're supposed to be resting!"

Matt leaned forward and gave Julie a kiss. His lips were moist, and Julie tasted a faint trace of toothpaste. "I promise, I'll just lie there like a good boy," Matt said. "And you can shower me with love and attention."

Julie laughed. "Typical."

"But irresistible, right?" Matt said. He kissed her again. Julie kissed him back, long and deep and sweet.

"Irresistible," she agreed. "Now go lie down, and I'll be in as soon as I wash up."

Matt grinned. "I love being sick in bed."

Two

Chiaroscuro. Chiaroscuro. Chiaroscuro. Seated at her desk in her divided double dorm room, Dahlia Sussman repeated the strange-sounding word over and over to herself, covering up the definition she'd written next to it in her notebook. She hoped that if she kept saying it, it would finally sink in. *Who knows?* she thought. *Maybe it will even start to mean something after a while.*

Dahlia shut her eyes tightly as she tried to recall the meaning of the word. *Chiaroscuro? Oh, yeah, it's a thick layer of paint or pigment,* she thought. She pulled her hand away from the notebook and peeked at the definition. Wrong.

"*Chiaroscuro, impasto, intonaco.* How in the world am I supposed to know which is which?" she said out loud.

If only Michelangelo had spoken English, Dahlia would have stood a chance. But the fact was that just a few weeks into the semester, she knew she was in deep trouble. Served her right for taking a class she wasn't supposed to be in in the first place.

Dahlia slammed her notebook shut and frowned at her hand-drawn cover. She'd made a little sketch of an Italian church, under which she'd written the course title—Art History/ Archaeology 351: An In-Depth Study of the Restoration of the Sistine Chapel. The 351 stood for advanced level, where Dahlia definitely didn't belong. She hadn't taken any of the introductory courses that were prerequisites for a higher-level class. At registration, she'd just checked the little box where it asked if she'd fulfilled all the requirements. Just like that, she'd promoted herself to advanced status.

And every day since, she had found herself struggling with new terms and theories, battling the most difficult reaches of art history and archaeology. The thick textbook that lay before her was bad enough. In class, she was sure her professor was speaking Italian, because she barely understood a word she said.

Dahlia felt like a fool for signing up for the class. But she was desperate. What else could she do? As much as she hated to admit it, she was still totally stuck on one Nick Stone. She'd found out he had signed up for the class, so she—well, she just signed up, too.

Julie's friend Nick.

That's all he'd been a few months ago when she'd offered him a ride back to New York during Thanksgiving break. Now she couldn't get him off her mind. Not even a wild, three-day fling with a cute guy in the Caribbean during winter break had helped her forget about Nick. Andrew what's-his-name was fine for a few days—if she couldn't have Nick. Andrew was cute and easy—and over.

Dahlia sat back and called up an image of Nick. Handsome, very. Tall, maybe a little on the thin side, but definitely well sculpted. Lean, that's what he was. With short, light-brown hair, gorgeous green eyes, and a knockout smile—the problem being that he just didn't direct that smile Dahlia's way. Nick wasn't just a hunk, he was interesting, too. He seemed to take things seriously, his life and the world around him. And he didn't just talk, he actually did things. Like working in a soup kitchen in New York City. He'd taken the train in from his parents' house in Westchester after Thanksgiving and Christmas to help serve food to the needy. And the summer before, while Dahlia and most of the people she knew from the city were busy getting the perfect tan, Nick was working in New Mexico on an archaeological dig.

Practically everything about him seemed so different from the guys Dahlia was used to. There was nothing spoiled and selfish about Nick. He didn't have a million-dollar bank account to fall back on whenever he got in a jam, like most of the kids Dahlia had grown up with on the Upper East Side of New York City.

Dahlia looked out her dorm window, hoping she'd catch a glimpse of him as she had yesterday. *I'm hopeless,* she thought. True enough, she knew she was hooked. For the first time in her life she wanted something badly and couldn't just have it. No, Dahlia couldn't smile in his direction and have him in the palm of her hand. In fact, the harder she tried, the more he seemed to think she was just a rich girl who needed to be the center of attention. But she was determined to prove him wrong. She didn't have any other choice. Because no matter how hard Dahlia told herself to forget about the guy, her crush seemed to only get worse.

As she stared out the window she imagined being in Nick's arms. Just the two of them, alone, in a warm, dark place. Long, passionate kisses. Long, passionate caresses. Was he a great kisser? Julie said he was. Lucky her. In her one brief moment of doubt about Matt, she'd gotten to kiss the cutest guy on campus.

"Dahlia?" an all-too-familiar voice brought her out of her fantasy. "Dahlia?" From the other side of the thin wall that divided the dorm room, Cindi was chirping away. "How about that yoga session I promised you?" she asked.

Reluctantly, Dahlia turned around to see her roommate's overly cheerful, round head poking through the door. Her shoulder-length, straight black hair framed a porcelain face, with apple-pink cheeks, that was all dimples and gigantic pearly whites. Dahlia returned the toothpaste-commercial smile. "No, thanks, Cindi. Not now."

"Ya sure? It'd be good for you."

Dahlia shook her head and reopened her notebook, emphasizing the fact that she was busy studying. "Uh-uh, Cindi."

"Positive, Dahlia?" Cindi continued. "Half the fun of doing yoga is sharing it with a friend."

Dahlia shook her head again, trying to remain calm. "Maybe later, okay?" The last thing she wanted now was to have Cindi twist her up into a pretzel and share her cosmic life with Dahlia. Rhythmic breathing at four o'clock in the afternoon was not what Dahlia had come to college for.

"You're sure now?" Cindi asked. "A couple of nice long stretches might be just what you need."

Enough on the yoga already! Didn't she ever stop? Dahlia felt on the verge of snapping. But she gritted her teeth and managed a smile back in Cindi's direction. "Thanks anyway, Cindi. It's really sweet of you. But I really need to study. College, remember?" There followed an awkward moment with Cindi remaining frozen in place in the doorway. Was Dahlia supposed to feel guilty?

The typical nightmare roommate experience. Dahlia had been excited at the prospect of having somebody new to room with this semester, thinking it might even be somebody as great as Julie. No such luck. Cindi, double emphasis on the "i" at the end, was like a cross between a Barbie doll and a New Age guru. Since day one of the new semester when Cindi had popped her head in and said "hi," it seemed as if Dahlia hadn't had a moment off from Cindi's Miss Congeniality routine.

If it wasn't yoga, it was "Hey, you want to borrow some of my healing crystals? Amethyst is supposed to be great for Virgos." Cindi's crystals were dangling from her ceiling on the other side of the divided double, which is exactly where Dahlia intended them to stay. Nutrition was another of Cindi's areas of expertise. She knew her vitamins. A for this, E for that, bee pollen and slow-absorption iron tablets for everything else. No question about it, Cindi from St. Louis was the friendliest, most dedicated roommate a girl could ask for, and Dahlia couldn't stand her.

"Hey, Cindi—" Dahlia said, a trace of annoyance sneaking into her voice, "I really do have to catch up on my homework, okay?"

"Yeah—sure, okay." She looked disappointed. "I'll be down the hall in the lounge if you need me for anything. See you later. Hey, maybe we'll go to dinner together tonight?"

"Sure." Dahlia nodded. "See you later."

Dahlia breathed a temporary sigh of relief as Cindi extra-politely shut the door behind her. Later—like much! Two hours till dinner. Dahlia wondered if she'd really have an entire one hundred and twenty minutes of freedom.

She glanced back down at her textbook. *The Sistine Chapel: Erasing or Restoring History?* Dahlia shrugged. How was she going to get through this course? When she'd signed up, she'd figured that her three visits to the Sistine Chapel in Rome, in person, would be enough to ace the class. She'd seen Michelangelo's masterpiece ceiling in all its phases—before, during, and after its historic cleaning. She knew just what it looked like. But in college, it seemed that actually being there was a far cry from reading about it. It seemed strange, somehow, that in books there was always so much more to learn.

Hopelessly, Dahlia tried to get through chapter one, underlining, scribbling in the margins, and making question marks after every second or third sentence. *Chiaroscuro.* That word kept popping up, and Dahlia kept failing to commit it to memory. It was no use. She tried to focus on the reading, but her mind kept wandering back to Nick, her whole reason for getting involved with this mess of a course.

Where was he now? Did she have any chance at all with him? Why was he so difficult to get, when practically every other guy in the past had been conquered so easily? How was she going to get him to really notice her? There had to be a way.

As Dahlia glanced at her bare hands, still showing a trace of bronze from her week in the Caribbean, she got an idea. In half an hour, lap swimming began at the gym pool, and she was pretty sure Nick would be headed there. Surely he'd take notice a lot quicker if he saw her looking her hottest, in the new string bikini she'd bought for her trip. Even if he gave her half the look she'd gotten from most other guys, that would be a start.

She thought back to several weeks ago, to all the stares she'd gotten from the guys on the beach in Guadeloupe. Heads had turned, eyes had followed her every step as she walked barefoot in the sand. When she'd noticed Andrew checking her out, all she had to do was smile at him, toss her long blond hair, and say "hi," and the next thing she knew he was walking alongside her, flirting up a storm. The more she thought about it, the more sure she was that Nick would have to notice her at the pool.

As she got up and went to her dresser to find the bikini, she felt the strangeness of her infatuation taking hold. The Sistine Chapel? String bikinis in the gym pool? Today, she'd even taken a double dose of Cindi's bee pollen, hoping it would actually make her healthier, happier, and therefore more desirable. Was she really doing all this for Nick? Could Nick possibly be worth it?

Dahlia gave herself a quick once-over in the mirror. Big blue eyes, long blond hair, and a habit of getting what she wanted. He'd be worth it. She was sure of it.

Three

"Cough. Again. Again. Good."

Matt sat on the examining table, following Dr. Zinn's instructions. Coughing was easy for Matt. He'd been doing it without any encouragement for the past month.

The doctor pressed a thumb firmly against Matt's chest. "Cough," he said again. "Uh-huh. Again. Hmm? Again."

Matt let out a harsh, hefty cough. Dr. Zinn continued to push his thumb against Matt's chest, throat, back, and neck, pressing, pinching, tapping. The doctor was being far more thorough today than he had been on Matt's first visit.

When he'd come to see him last month, the doctor had merely felt his head with the back of his hand and said, "Hot," looked down his throat and said, "Red," and then took his temperature and told him he had the flu, like everybody else in Ohio. "Nothing a few days in Florida wouldn't cure," he'd joked.

Matt felt the pressure of the doctor's hand on the side of his neck. "Does that hurt?" he asked, pressing simultaneously against Matt's neck and right lung.

Matt shook his head.

"How 'bout that?" he asked, pressing his finger a little deeper into Matt's neck.

"Nope," Matt said.

"Well, one thing's for sure," Dr. Zinn said as he let go of Matt's neck. "It's pretty darned hard to hurt you. What are you made of, anyway?"

Matt laughed. "So I'm okay, then?" he asked, expecting to see Dr. Zinn nod.

He didn't. "Well, I guess if you were okay, you wouldn't have come back to see me in the first place, right?"

Matt nodded, feeling a little confused by the doctor's evasiveness. "So . . ."

Dr. Zinn paused. He scratched the back of his head, as if searching for words. "So it's my job to tell you what you've got that's making you not okay. Only I'm afraid that I'm not really sure what it is yet."

"You mean you don't know?"

The doctor smiled. It was the kind of smile

that said "don't worry" and "there's a problem," all at the same time. "Matt, why don't you get dressed and meet me in my office in five, okay? We'll talk there."

"Sure," Matt said, immediately beginning to worry. He hurriedly threw his clothes on. Something was wrong, that much was clear.

When Matt stepped into the office, Dr. Zinn was sitting behind a big wooden desk that was piled high with medical texts, stacks of X rays, and lots of papers scribbled with notes. Matt noticed one note, written in red Magic Marker. *Rachel's birthday Friday. Don't forget!* it read.

Dr. Zinn tapped a pencil on the desktop, his eyes scanning the notes he'd taken while examining Matt. "Sit down," he said, pointing to a leather chair across from him.

Matt sat, waiting for the doctor to speak. He thought of Julie, who had been bugging him for the last few weeks to see the doctor again. He hadn't even told her he'd made today's appointment, not wanting to worry her. But now, he was the one who felt worried.

As he studied Dr. Zinn, Matt was glad to be in his care. The doctor was young, with a neatly trimmed beard and dark, curly hair. The beard made his boyish face look a little older, but the college student in him—he'd graduated from Madison less than ten years ago—was still apparent. Dr. Zinn seemed friendly, relaxed, even funny, yet, at the same time, concerned and serious. Looking at him right now, though, his brow creased, Matt wished he didn't look quite so serious.

"Okay," the doctor finally said. "It's like this, Matt." He exhaled a heavy breath of air. "There most definitely is something wrong with you. You've got a lump in your neck."

Matt's hand went immediately to the side of his neck, to the place the doctor had been pressing on earlier. Sure enough, his fingers found a hard lump the size of a large pea. "Whoa! What is that?" Matt hadn't even noticed it before.

"Well, it's possible it's nothing at all," Dr. Zinn replied. "Nothing serious, I mean."

"Possible?" Matt felt for the lump again.

"You may very well have had the flu a month ago, but that's not the case now. What I found are severely swollen lymph nodes. That's the lump in the side of your neck. As I said, it may be nothing serious," Dr. Zinn repeated. "But there is a slight chance—"

He paused before saying the word that made Matt's blood run cold. "—that it's cancer. Cancer. I'm afraid there is the slight possibility that what you have in there is growing rapidly, infecting the cells around it. Just a possibility," he emphasized. "Slight, but something we need to look into."

Matt barely heard the rest of what Dr. Zinn said. Cancer? Him? But he was one of the healthiest, strongest people he knew. All he had was a hacking cough. Cancer was something people died from.

"We'll know for sure after we run the necessary tests," Dr. Zinn was saying. He told Matt that the tests would be extensive, and that they'd need to do a biopsy, which would land him in the hospital for a few days. "We remove the lump and analyze it. I'll bet you could use a few days off from work anyway, a couple days of R and R."

Tests? Hospital? Time off from work? None of it was really making sense yet. Matt took a deep breath and exhaled heavily. "Wow. It sounds pretty scary. When would I have the tests?"

"As soon as possible, Matt. No time like the present with something like this. My secretary will help you make hospital arrangements."

It all seemed to be happening too fast. Matt wished Julie could be here now. She'd be a lot better at taking it all in than he was. She was the sensible half of the family. "Dr. Zinn," Matt said, "before I make all the plans, I think I need to talk to Julie about everything. I mean—"

"I understand, Matt. I'm sure this is a lot for you to think about all at once." He smiled. "You can have her call me, if there's anything she needs to know."

"Thanks." Matt knew the doctor was being as comforting as possible. But somehow he still felt totally confused.

"Matt, the tests are nothing to be afraid of. You need them. It's the only way to find out what's going on inside there. This may sound silly, Matt, but you shouldn't worry," he said. He shook Matt's hand while rising. "Whatever it is, it's good we caught it now."

"Sure, I guess," Matt said, reaching for his neck again.

"A few things you should know," the doctor said. "First, I meant it when I said it's probably nothing serious. And second, if it is serious, it's treatable, and I'll be with you all the way."

Matt managed a smile. "Thanks. But it's going to be hard not to worry. I think I'm feeling sicker, just since you said that word." Cancer. Matt couldn't even say it.

Dr. Zinn patted Matt on the shoulder. "You seem like a smart boy, Matt. You don't worry till you see me start worrying."

"It's just a lump, huh? Nothing serious?" Matt asked, trying to forget the "C" word.

"Let's hope so." The doctor smiled reassuringly.

Marion Green leaned against the wall just

outside her dorm room, closed her eyes, puckered up, and enjoyed five soft, tender kisses on her lips.

"There. One sweet kiss for every hour that's passed since I last saw you."

Marion giggled. Fred Fryer was the sweetest, there was no doubt about it. And she loved the way he kissed.

Fred leaned closer and kissed her again.

"What's that one for?" she asked.

Fred shrugged. "I don't know. I just couldn't resist," he said.

Marion ran a hand through Fred's wavy red hair. "I'll let you give me one more kiss. Then let's go get some lunch, okay? I'm starving."

"Your lips are all the nourishment I'll ever need," Fred said, his face close to Marion's. She felt his warmth, and, as hungry as she was for lunch, found herself happily giving in to him. She closed her eyes and pressed her body close to his.

"Ooooh-eeee. Hot and heavy." Marion heard a voice trail down the hall. It wasn't the first time she and Fred had been caught this way in public. "Don't they ever stop?" the voice continued. Marion was pretty sure that it was Sarah Pike.

"So much for being shy!" Marion didn't have to look to know that Gwen was with Sarah. In a way, Marion had Gwen to thank for the very kisses Fred was showering her with now. It was Gwen who had helped Marion to figure out a way to stop Fred from chickening out every time they were alone together. "Just go get him! Take charge!" she'd told Marion back in the fall. "How can he resist?"

Sure enough, ever since that famous first kiss in the art museum sculpture garden, there'd been no stopping Fred. As Gwen had pointed out, Fred had been cured forever. And Marion finally had her first boyfriend.

She blushed as she heard Gwen and Sarah's giggles fade into the distance. "Fred! Everybody's watching."

"Oops, sorry, Marion. I can't help it. I keep getting carried away." Fred smiled adoringly at her. His freckled face was irresistible.

Marion reached up on tiptoe and kissed the tip of his nose. "Come on, Fred," she said, taking his hand and starting down the hall. "Let's eat."

"Okay," Fred agreed. "But I know what I'd like for dessert," he said, arching an eyebrow.

"Boys," Marion groaned. "One-track minds." Not that she wasn't looking forward to another sweet kiss after lunch, too. Still, she reminded herself that this afternoon's dessert kiss would be a short one. Not like yesterday, when their lips had remained locked so long, they'd missed biology lab. Marion's first skipped class of her life had been awfully fun. *But not today,* she promised herself. One kiss, and they'd head off to class.

Four

Julie doodled in the margin of her journalism notebook. As Professor Copeland lectured about the fine line between human-interest stories and sensationalism, she drew a single eye next to her notes with her new turquoise pen. The lashes were long and exaggerated, and a plump teardrop fell from one corner. Julie heaved a silent sigh and crossed out the teardrop with a decisive X. She wasn't going to start getting all depressed. She and Matt had decided to stay optimistic, think positive.

Yeah, right. Think positive, when the word *biopsy* was echoing in her brain. Julie shivered. *Biopsy . . . malignancy, cancer . . . death.* A nightmare domino chain of words.

Julie drew one of those dumb happy faces—a circle with two dots for eyes and a big smile.

Everything's going to be fine, she tried to tell herself. Too many tearjerkers on TV lately. She was probably just overreacting.

But what if she wasn't? What if Matt went into the hospital and . . . Julie felt a tightness in her chest and throat. She knew what it was like to lose someone she loved. Her sister had died over two years ago. Matt could be next. The horror building inside her spiraled. She'd never stop missing Mary Beth, never stop wondering what her sister's life would have been like if she'd lived.

The image of Mary Beth's charred car, the front end crumpled around a thick tree like a piece of aluminum foil, swelled unbearably in her mind's eye. Julie's whole body was seized with pain and sorrow—even now, two-and-a-half years later. How could she ever go through anything like that again? How could she bear to be without the most important person in the world?

Julie rocked back and forth in her chair. *Please let Matt be okay,* she thought. *Please.* He couldn't be sick. He was so strong and healthy. She pictured the well-defined muscles of his smooth body. The smile that was so full of life. Matt, sick? Impossible. Matt wouldn't leave her alone. He couldn't.

And if he did? Julie shuddered as she imagined herself in their little apartment, Matt's clothes and belongings only a reminder that he was gone. Who would be there for her? Her parents? Since Mary Beth's death, her family had grown more and more distant. And by deciding to marry Matt, Julie had only made things worse. Much worse.

"You're on your own now," Dad had said, in place of congratulations. And her mother might have paid Julie's most recent tuition bill, but she'd done it secretly, silently, without saying a word to Julie about it, as if helping out her married daughter was something she had to be ashamed about. If it weren't for the letters from her twelve-year-old brother, Tommy, Julie reflected unhappily, it would almost feel as if she didn't have a family.

Wait. Scratch that. Matt was her family. Julie touched the triple wedding bands on her ring finger. Past, present, and—and what? The biopsy, the hospital tests. Past, present, and "if." An awful, terrifying "if."

"Ms. Miller?" Professor Copeland's testy voice was almost a welcome relief from Julie's thoughts. "Are you getting all this down?" He peered at her notebook, the margin full of turquoise doodles, her pen poised absently above the paper.

Julie looked up at him, embarrassed.

"Nothing serious, Ms. Miller. Just the instructions for one of your first big assignments of the semester. You'll have to get the information from one of your classmates. Though if this were the real world, I doubt your colleagues would be so helpful. If you were supposed to report on, let's say, a five-alarm fire, and you missed the address, well, someone would probably tell you the fire was in Cleveland—when, in fact, it was in Chicago!"

"Sorry," Julie answered meekly.

As Professor Copeland turned away from Julie, John Graham leaned across the aisle. "Hey," he whispered, his mane of long red-blond hair falling across his face. "I'll fill you in after class."

"Thanks," Julie whispered back. For the rest of the period, she tried to focus on Professor Copeland's lecture. But she couldn't stop thinking about Matt. *Please be fine,* she wished fervently. *Please.*

She drew a heart on her notebook. She and Matt were together forever. Forever. That had to mean a long, long time.

"Four burgers all the way and a double order of fries—table nine," Matt called out to Pat through the opening that separated the kitchen from the restaurant.

"Got it," Pat shouted back frantically over the music. There were at least a dozen burgers still on the grill, and three huge vats of french fries were cooking. She put a platter of fries on an already stacked tray and handed it to Matt. "These are for Marcy's table. Sure you can get it all at once, Matt?" she asked, her voice filled with motherly concern, even though she was only a few years older than Matt.

"I'm fine, Pat, really," Matt insisted. He raised the tray high overhead and wove his way through the crowd.

Club Night was just getting under way at the Barn and Grill, and it was already rocking, big-time rocking. Matt glanced up into the hayloft at the front. Up above, bathed in cool blue light, Leon "the Lip" wailed on the saxophone. At first, Matt could tell the audience thought it was pretty weird to have a solo performer on Club Night. But Leon was showing everyone that he could play the blues just fine all on his own. He made his sax sing, and he'd captivated the audience with an exciting range of sounds—from lilting, melodious moans to somber sighs, to high-frequency, piercing shouts. Matt had heard Leon play enough at his apartment to know he was good, but somehow, the live audience combined with the wash of stage lights made Leon sound that much better.

As Matt glanced over at the front door, he

noticed a line of people waiting to get in. He smiled proudly. If Club Night continued to be such a success, there was no telling how far he could take it. Before long he'd be booking world-class names. Maybe he'd even start his own club. Matt could imagine the proud look on his father's face when he found out his son had become the biggest rock-and-roll promoter in the Midwest.

For now, though, it was exciting enough to be a full-time waiter and part-time promoter. He set the tray down on Marcy's table and started serving burgers and fries to everyone. "Who gets the rare with Swiss?" he asked.

"That's okay, Matt, just leave them on the table." Marcy placed a bill in his hand and gently pushed his arm away. "We'll figure 'em all out, honey." The others nodded as they reached for their platters.

Matt tried not to show the frustration that was building inside. But once again, he'd received special treatment from the concerned citizens of Madison, Ohio.

They all knew. Matt was always aware that news traveled fast in a small town, and especially in a small college town. He and Julie had barely told anyone directly, but the Madison grapevine had spread the word: Announcement, Matt is sick.

But why were so many people treating him

with kid gloves? The biopsy wasn't until Monday. Dr. Zinn had told him how little chance there was of something being seriously wrong with him. But somehow, the others felt differently. It was as if they'd already condemned Matt to die.

People were tipping him big, for little or no work. They looked at him with faces of concern, and even sorrow. Wasn't Pat busy enough behind the grill? Did she have to be so eager to offer help serving? "That's okay, buddy, I'll get it from Jake at the bar," one of his regulars had told him earlier, patting him gingerly on the back as if Matt might break.

On the other hand, there were the ones who were so freaked out by the word *biopsy* that they couldn't even face Matt. Like Jake, for one. Matt had always thought of him as being totally together, able to handle whatever came his way. With Pat's help, Jake had turned a crumbling, drafty barn into Madison's most popular bar and restaurant. But when it came to dealing with Matt's illness, Jake couldn't even admit that something was wrong. "Oh, I'm sure you're fine" was all he could manage when Matt told him he'd need a few days off for the hospital stay. How could Jake be sure when Dr. Zinn wasn't?

Matt swallowed hard. He wanted to take a few big breaths and go on with his life. But it wasn't so easy when people around him were making him even more worried. Matt had been totally pumped for Club Night, only to find half the place already had him six feet under. And maybe the other half just hadn't heard yet.

As he started back toward the kitchen, he noticed that Pat had filled another tray with food and was about to deliver it herself. He hurried over to the counter. "Hey, I thought that was my job, Pat." He started to take the tray away from her, but he could sense her resistance.

"No problem, Matt," Pat said. "The grill's practically empty. Relax, take five. Enjoy Club Night. It's your baby."

"Pat—"

"That's an order, Matt," she insisted. "I'm still your boss, remember?"

Matt shrugged. "Fine. But I'm back on the job in five minutes. I'll be over at Julie's table if you need me, okay?"

Julie, her dark hair spilling over her shoulders, was sitting at a big round table with a whole gang of people from school. Matt recognized everybody except the girl sitting next to Dahlia's friend, Paul Chase.

"What does everybody think of Leon?" Matt asked as he approached the table. He gave Julie a loving squeeze on the shoulder and bent down to kiss her on the cheek. "Hi."

"A little hard to dance to, but he's really wild. I knew there was a reason you and Leon got along so well," Julie said. She took hold of Matt's hand and gave it an extra-hard squeeze.

Matt pulled up a chair from another table and sat down. He couldn't help noticing all the heightened reactions. The love on Julie's round face was tinged with worry. Dahlia's blue eyes were wide with intense concern. Marion wore the same worried expression as Pat. Fred was scrutinizing him, as if Matt were a science experiment and he was checking him out for visible signs of sickness. Sarah and Gwen both smiled nervously, and Paul's eyes seemed to be looking everywhere but at Matt. Only the attractive, dark-skinned girl at his side smiled comfortably at Matt with her friendly, almond-shaped eyes.

"Hey, do you like the music?" Matt asked her.

"I think he's great. I love your Club Night idea, too. Finally, something happening to do in this town." She extended her hand. "I'm Maya."

"She's from L.A., capital of happening," Paul said, wrapping his arm around her shoulder. "I—I'm sorry, Matt, I should have introduced you two."

"It's okay," Matt said. He couldn't help but notice the awkwardness in Paul's voice, but decided it best to just ignore it.

"You know we're all pulling for you, Matt," Dahlia said. "Big time."

"Good luck on Monday," Fred and Marion said simultaneously.

There was a brief moment of silence.

"Hey, Matt," Maya said, leaning across Paul toward him. "I'm sure you'll be fine. Things have a way of turning out for the best when you really want them to."

Matt felt a giant wave of relief wash over him. Finally, someone was making a little bit of sense. Maybe Paul's friend did have the mellow, California attitude, but as far as Matt was concerned, he wished a few of the others did, too.

"Thanks," he said. He saw a smile light up Julie's brown eyes. "You know, actually I didn't have any plans to get really sick. I figured with Club Night just taking off and everything, I'd better stay healthy."

Julie raised an eyebrow. "How about staying healthy for me, too?"

Matt leaned over and gave her a kiss on the lips. "I'm here for the long haul, Jules. But I'd better get back to work. Got to make some money."

As he said good-bye to everybody, he noticed their looks of worry hadn't quite gone away. Well, if they wanted a cancer patient for a friend, they weren't going to get one. Not Matt, anyway. No way, he was just fine.

He *was* fine. Sure, there was still a little doubt in his own mind. Maybe more than a little. But Monday's tests would do away with all of it. Matt let out a deep breath. He was pushing ahead. Life was for living.

Five

Julie sat on the edge of Matt's hospital bed, holding his hand. His cheeks were pink and healthy-looking, his hair dark against the white linen and drab green walls. He looked totally adorable for a guy in a hospital gown. Except for the bandage on the side of his neck, he didn't look a bit like he belonged here.

"Man, this one test hurt like crazy," he was saying. "They put a needle right into my spine."

Julie cringed, feeling an imaginary pinch in her own spine. "I can't even think about it."

Matt shrugged easily. "It was the worst one. The biopsy—" he pointed at his neck, "well, I was out for that, so I didn't feel a thing. But, wow, trying to wake up from the anesthesia was really strange. It was like I was having all these weird dreams—all these ghost sort of people floating around and bells going off—and I start to realize it's really the doctors and nurses and the sounds of the hospital, only I can't get anything into focus and I can't figure out what anyone's saying." Matt coughed. "I can't believe I'm finally awake."

"Well, you look fine. Better than fine," Julie said, bringing Matt's hand to her mouth and kissing his fingers. Thank goodness the tests were over. Now all they had to do was wait for the results to confirm that he was okay. How could anyone who looked so healthy—and cute—be sick?

"I'll be finer when I get out of this place," Matt said. "Man, you wonder how anyone can get better around here. They're running in and out of the room all night, taking your temperature and making you swallow pills, and they're paging doctors over the intercoms—you can't get a good night's sleep. And that guy snores like a buzz saw." Matt jabbed his thumb at the empty bed next to him. His roommate, who'd just had shoulder surgery, was downstairs in physical therapy.

"Plus the food is about the furthest thing from healthy," Matt went on. "At first, I was totally psyched when they took the I.V. tube out of my arm and I could eat again, but look." He reached over to his night table for a small, heavy piece of paper and handed it to Julie.

"Dinner," Julie read. "Check one. Chicken à la king or creamed beef."

"Mystery meat with goop," Matt translated.

"Peas, corn, or carrots."

"Cooked to a tasteless pulp. And for the big highlight of your meal, a dish of Jell-O! Par-ty!"

Julie laughed. "Sounds like what I have to serve at the dining hall. Maybe they have some big central underground kitchen and pipes running to all the institutional cafeterias—"

"Like a sewer system," Matt put in. "As a matter of fact . . ."

"Gross, Matt!" Julie shook her head. "But speaking of sewers, get a load of Copeland's big assignment this semester. We're supposed to read some article they published in the *Register* a while back about a proposed pooper-scooper law in Madison. Copeland said he thought it was the worst-written article in the history of journalism. Anyway, we're supposed to research the issue and write our own articles. Talk about dumb."

"Pooper-scooper. You mean, like cleaning up after your dog?" Matt asked.

Julie nodded. "Yup. Half my final grade depends on it. Can you believe it? I mean, there are people out there dying, and we've got to write about dog poop!"

Suddenly, she realized what she'd said. *People dying.* The words lay on the sterile, medicinal-smelling hospital air. She felt her body tense up. Her eyes met Matt's. They held each other's gaze for a long, silent moment.

"Hey," Matt said softly. "You're the one who said I look better than fine." Julie heard the note of fear that surfaced in his voice.

She squeezed his hand harder. "You do," she said fiercely. "So why don't they tell you—tell us?"

"Dr. Zinn said it would take a while to get the results." Matt frowned. "I never was much good at surprises. I just want to get out of this place and get back to what counts. Hey, did I tell you I'm trying to get the X-Tones to come play at Club Night?" The change of subject seemed to restore his confidence.

Julie knew enough to follow his lead. "You've told me at least three times already." She laughed. "The X-Tones would be great."

She and Matt stuck to safe subjects, navigating away from the waiting and worry over Matt's test results. But it was close to impossible to forget about that with the bustling of nurses and orderlies in the hall outside the open door—pushing carts or rushing to administer medicine, the smell of disinfectant, the sudden burst of a voice coming through the speaker over Matt's bed.

"Paging Dr. Plumber. Dr. Plumber, room six-oh-three, immediately." *This is a place of ur-*

gency, emergency, and sickness, Julie thought. Matt didn't belong here.

Matt must have sensed her tension. He grabbed hold of her hand. "So . . . tell me about all the great things you've been up to while I've been trying to decide between the gross chicken and the disgusto beef."

Julie tried to laugh, tried to make an effort to push her worry aside. "Well, we started the *Oresteia* in Classics. See, there's this royal family—King Agamemnon and Queen Clytemnestra and their kids, Orestes, Electra, and Iphigenia. They've all got this family curse on them from way back when the great-great-grandfather stole his brother's wife, so the brother boiled up the first guy's children and served them to him for dinner."

Matt made a face, accompanied by his cough. "Wow, I'll take that Jell-O, thank you very much."

Julie laughed. "Yeah, it's a little more intense than dog poop."

"Sounds like some ancient Greek soap opera," Matt commented. "Better than *Children's Hospital* and that stupid emergency-rescue show." He nodded with his chin at the television anchored up above his bed. "I mean, what a choice for someone in this place."

"Well, you can read the plays when I'm done with them," Julie said. "Anyway, after Classics, I went to the library for a while and then I worked the lunch shift. Fred and Marion came through the line. They said to say hi and that they're thinking of you. Dahlia, too. She said to give you a big smooch. Then—I came over here."

Julie decided to leave out how she'd run into Nick after work and had gone to get a cup of coffee with him at the snack bar. A totally innocent cup of coffee. Still, she knew Matt didn't need to hear about it. Not now.

"Well?" Matt arched a dark eyebrow.

Oh, no. Could Matt see there was something she wasn't telling him? Julie felt a stab of guilt—followed by a flutter of annoyance at herself. She hadn't done anything wrong. She and Nick had gabbed about classes and traded some campus gossip for a little while. The way they used to do—before. "Well, what?" she asked evenly.

"I thought you said Dahlia said to give me a big smooch."

"Oh. Yeah, of course." Julie leaned toward Matt and gave him a loud, noisy kiss on the cheek. "That's from Dahlia. And this is from me." She kissed him on the lips.

"Mmm. More," Matt murmured. He wrapped his arms around Julie and pulled her down next to him on the hospital bed. They kissed again. Warm, lingering, gentle, and hungry at the same time. Julie felt Matt stroking her head, her back. Her hands traced the contours of his arms and chest. He was naked under the thin hospital gown.

"Excuse me," a high, metallic voice barked. Julie twisted around to see a tall, thin, sour-faced nurse holding a thermometer attached by a cord to a small, computerized box.

"Oh, Nurse Rodriguez," Matt said. "Always a pleasure."

Nurse Rodriguez shook her head. "The patient is supposed to be resting. If I catch you breaking hospital policy again, the young lady is going to have to leave."

Julie sat up and straightened her shirt.

Matt looked at Julie and winked. "Yes, ma'am," he said, both of them holding back their laughter.

The image on the large screen at the front of the lecture hall depicted a group of naked angels, their bodies twisting and turning in all directions at once. "Pay close attention to the subtle variation in value and tone. You must study the coloration very carefully if you are to form your own opinion on the ceiling," came the Italian-accented woman's voice from the back of the classroom. The shadow of a pointer stick moved across the screen, stopping to highlight some of the details—a gray-brown section of a leg, a somber chestnut cheek, a blackened torso.

Dahlia tried to concentrate on the screen and scribble a few words into her notebook at the same time. Neither was easy to do when Nick was sitting right next to her. No matter how hard she tried, she couldn't keep from sneaking glances over her left shoulder throughout the slide lecture. With his fine features in an expression of concentration, he looked totally gorgeous in the shimmery glow from the projector.

Dahlia sighed. She felt even more in love than she had been back in junior high school, when she'd had a major thing for Chris Elgard, her first boyfriend. But she'd won Chris over without even trying. One flash of the famous Dahlia Sussman smile was all it took back then. Looking at Nick now, she knew it was going to take a lot more than a sexy smile. But there was no turning back. She was going to sit next to him all semester and, yes, she was going to get him, too.

"What you see here is the result of four hundred years of time. Incense, oil lamps, candles, the leaking roof, atrocious attempts at repainting and glazing, all these factors have contributed to what, until recently, we knew as Michelangelo's masterpiece, the Sistine Chapel. It is undoubtedly one of the greatest accomplishments by any artist in the history of the Western World. But what did it really look like when Michelangelo first painted it?" Ms. Godarotti spoke quickly and with great intensity. Dahlia thought of her teacher as being a direct descendant of the artist.

The screen flashed another picture of the same angels, this one appearing a little brighter and more colorful than the last. The pointer rested on an angel's thigh. What had been a dark, grayish brown in the previous picture was now many shades lighter, hints of red and orange becoming visible. "Stage one of the cleaning process. A simple solution of distilled water, baking soda, and ammonium bicarbonate, applied with a soft sponge." As the teacher went into fuller detail about the cleaning process, peppering her lecture with Italian names and phrases, Dahlia found herself focusing on Nick.

She loved the intensity with which he listened to the lecture. His eyes seemed to penetrate the screen, scanning for more details. His page was filled with notes and little drawings of the angels. There were question marks, exclamation marks, underlined words. Nick was a serious young man, and Dahlia was totally impressed. As the next slide was revealed on the screen, Dahlia saw Nick's face light up with fascination. So intense, yet so adorable.

She looked up to see the same angels on the screen, this time even brighter than before.

More pure reds and yellows, pinks and lavenders, and more variations of each color than before. Dahlia remembered seeing the ceiling that way when she and her parents had been in Rome at a special private showing of the ceiling while the cleaning was in progress. There had been a lot of debate then about how much further the restoration team should go. Many artists and historians were up in arms about erasing too much. Dahlia remembered one guy, an artist from New York, who was so convinced that the cleaning would destroy Michelangelo's shading and special varnishes, that he had to be physically removed from the chapel when he'd started shaking the scaffolding.

Class ended, and Ms. Godarotti announced that they'd continue the slide lecture next time. "Keep up with your reading, students. There's lots to learn about this masterpiece."

As the lights popped on, Dahlia flashed her best smile at Nick. "Great pictures, huh?"

"Uh-huh." He looked back down at his notebook and started writing. Wasn't the lecture over? She guessed there were still things on his mind that he wanted to get down.

Or maybe he was just trying his best to ignore her. Dahlia had decided to forget about their rotten start, during Thanksgiving break when she gave him a ride back to New York. The snowstorm, the breakdown, the fight they'd had. She'd forgiven Nick. But she wondered if the bad feelings were still fresh in his mind. He finished scribbling and shut his notebook.

She quickly shut hers, too, hoping he didn't see how little she'd written in it. "So—" she said. She tried extra hard to start something, anything. "What do you think?"

"You mean about the use of ammonium bicarbonate?"

Dahlia gulped. Ammonium what? "Uh—yeah," she managed.

"Pretty intense argument, that's for sure. I guess there's lots of reading to do to figure it all out. But it seems a little farfetched to think that a simple salt solution could destroy the painting."

Wow. Three whole sentences. Dahlia felt as if she'd actually broken through. "Four hundred and seventy-five years of grime. Imagine being the one to do the cleaning."

"You mean because they were right up there, close to the source of the inspiration? Pretty amazing, huh?"

"Yeah, that's what I meant," Dahlia said. *Not.* But if she just sort of nodded, maybe Nick would think they were on the same wavelength.

"I'm just really glad they let me take this class. You know, I haven't taken any art history yet, just archaeology, so I had to practically beg my way in," Nick said. "Did you have her last semester for Intro to Art History? I think she's great."

Dahlia shook her head. She was afraid to admit that she'd just sort of checked the little box that asked about prerequisites on the registration sign-up sheet, even though she hadn't fulfilled the requirements.

"I guess the really big thing is all about how the cleaning affected the *chiaroscuro,*" Nick said.

Dahlia's mouth was instantly open wide, hanging there long enough to expose her as a fraud. That word again. It had come back to haunt her. What the heck did it mean? She could feel herself turning bright red. "Um . . . well, I suppose . . ."

"You know, the shading. All those intricate forms created with lights and darks. Didn't you study the Renaissance in Intro?" Nick's eyes seemed to waver between inquisitive and accusing.

Dahlia knew it was time to confess. "Well, actually this is my first art-history class," she said, wrapping her finger nervously around a lock of her blond hair. "I mean, well, I was really interested in the class."

"So you just signed up?" Nick rolled his eyes, dismissing her as the fake that she was.

"Yeah. Well, I figured I could handle it. I've seen the ceiling three times."

"Seen it? Like, in person seen it?" Nick whistled.

Oops. Dahlia couldn't tell if he was impressed, envious, or just plain disdainful. Why had she let it slip about her trips to Rome? Now Nick was going to be more convinced than ever that she was just a spoiled, rich kid. She gathered up her books and slid them into her black canvas shoulder bag.

"Three times?" Nick asked, piling up his books and picking them up in his arms. "So did you get to see the ceiling before and after the renovation?"

Dahlia nodded, shooting him a sidelong glance. What do you know. He actually seemed to be interested! *Come on, Sussman,* she told herself. *The ball's in your court now.*

"And during, too," she said. "That was the most exciting time of all, when it was half new and half old. You know that picture that was on the screen at the end of class? Well, that was sort of what the ceiling looked like back when all the arguing was going on about whether to continue the restoration."

"Yeah? Wow, what I'd give to have seen that," Nick said. "You're lucky."

"Yeah, well . . ."

"So you're an expert, then," Nick said. "I

mean, you're probably the only person in all of Ohio who has actually seen the ceiling in all three phases. Even Ms. Godarotti said she hasn't seen it since the restoration. That makes you our own private authority."

Dahlia laughed. "I never really thought of it like that. I suppose you're right."

"So what's our local expert's take on the restoration? Was it worth it?" Nick asked. His serious expression from before was fading, a smile beginning to soften his face.

Flirting. Dahlia was sure that Nick was actually flirting with her. She definitely didn't mind it a bit. "Well, that time I was in Rome, when they were in the middle, I remember thinking how fresh and polished the already restored parts were. It seemed to make sense. Until I looked at the old stuff. It was like they'd erased a lot of the mystery. The romance was gone," she said.

"Hmmmm." Nick looked a little puzzled. "No more romance, huh? But instead, you could see the whole thing for what it was, right? Clean and fresh and colorful."

"Yeah. Well, no," Dahlia corrected herself. "I mean, I don't know, really."

"Sounds to me like the only ones who really wanted the ceiling left alone were the hopeless romantics," Nick said, rolling his eyes.

"Maybe, Nick. But I don't see what's so

great about a squeaky-clean ceiling if they take the heart and soul out of it."

"Hopeless romantic," Nick said again. Dahlia couldn't tell if he was teasing or annoyed.

"Maybe." Dahlia let out a sigh. If only Nick was a little more romantic. Toward her. Was he flirting, or wasn't he? "Rome's a beautiful city," she said, trying to keep the conversation going.

"I'll bet. Crazy place, too, I hear."

"Yeah, it's pretty wild. You spend half your life in a restaurant or café. And dinner doesn't start till ten at least. Nobody sleeps. They just drink another cappuccino."

"Yeah, my parents went there on a sort of second honeymoon. They were boring us with slides for weeks afterward, but you could tell they had a pretty great time."

The idea of a little escape to Rome with Nick wasn't such a horrible thought. One minute in such a romantic city would be all she'd need with him, and he'd be hers forever. Walking past all the fountains and the little squares, holding hands . . .

"Hey, listen," Nick said. "I was wondering if you've heard anything from Julie."

"Julie?" Good-bye Rome, homemade pasta, and crazy, late nights near the Colosseum. She frowned. Nick didn't still have a thing for Julie, did he?

"About Matt," he said. The serious Nick had taken over. No more fun, no more flirting. "Any word about his tests?"

"Oh." And just like that, reality had returned. Dahlia shrugged. "Still no word. You know, they did those tests nearly a week ago. I know Matt's been calling the doctor at least twice a day."

"Yeah, I would be, too," Nick said. Dahlia could see the concern on Nick's face was real, despite the fact that Matt wouldn't give him the time of day anymore.

"I'm sure Matt's going to be fine. I just saw him yesterday at their place. He was antsy, but he looked great. You know Matt, he's a fighter."

"Yeah," Nick said, a note of remorse in his voice.

"Want me to tell him you were asking about him?" Dahlia asked.

"Sure. I guess. Okay." He paused a moment, then looked away. "Well, I'm heading this way," Nick said, pointing toward a wing of professors' offices. "I'll see you in class on Friday."

They said good-bye. Dahlia felt a slight sting of rejection. Why did he have to end the conversation so abruptly? She wished he'd stay and hang out with her. What about lunch? Didn't the guy eat? They'd finally managed to get past the fighting stage. Okay, so they didn't exactly agree on the Sistine Chapel, but it made for conversation, at least. But then, just like that, it was over. See you later.

As Dahlia watched Nick walk away, she could hear Paul Chase's voice inside her head. "Just forget the guy, will you? If he doesn't see how great you are, then he doesn't deserve you."

She let out a heavy sigh. *Not yet, Paul. Not yet,* she thought. Julie said that Dahlia's attraction stemmed from the challenge of Nick's being so out of reach. But what about his eyes, the intensity of his face, even the way his hand moved across the page when he took notes? Dahlia felt certain that it was more than that.

Six

It was the most unextraordinary afternoon in the world. Julie stood at her window and stared outside. Out on the Green, a couple of students were having a snowball fight. A car was driving slowly down Main Street, and behind it rolled a delivery truck. A woman in a navy ski jacket and red knit hat was coming out of Gibson's Bakery with a little girl who clutched a white paper bag. Looking in the display window down the block at Books and Things was a tall, thin boy Julie had seen a few times at the library.

Just another day in Madison, Ohio. *Nothing out of the ordinary can happen today,* Julie told herself. Everything was the way it was supposed to be. She turned from the window and paced up and down her small living room, listening for the sound of Matt's motorcycle. On a day like this, how could he come home from the doctor's office with bad news?

Julie had wanted to go with him, to hold his hand as Dr. Zinn gave them the results of Matt's hospital tests, but Matt had said he'd be fine on his own. "You don't want to go skipping classes to sit around my doctor's office," he'd said. "You've got a life to live—and so do I." Julie hadn't missed the extra edge of insistence in Matt's voice, an insistence that he needed to act as if everything were normal.

But as the metallic roar of Matt's bike cut the air, every nerve, every muscle in Julie's body was on alert. She'd been practically holding her breath for a week, waiting to find out the results of those hospital tests. She rushed back to the window. There he was, riding up the block. She felt her heart skip a beat. Matt—in his jeans and leather jacket, thick-gloved hands on the handles of the bike. She watched, her breath held, as he braked to a stop, cut the engine, and threw a blue-jeaned leg over the bike to dismount. Same as always. Everything had to be fine.

Julie knew his next move. Her eyes followed him as he reached up to take off his helmet. She waited to see his expression, the moment stretching tense and thin. He raised the shiny black shell up and shook out his hair. He turned toward the door of their building.

Julie looked down from their second-floor apartment. Matt's face was blank, unreadable. Her heart pounded. Matt glanced up toward the window. He caught sight of Julie waiting there and waved, his mouth forming a little smile. But his smile looked unsteady.

Julie breathed in sharply. As Matt reached the downstairs entrance, she whirled away from the window and rushed to the door of their apartment. She felt queasy. She pulled open the door and raced down the stairs to meet him.

Julie threw her arms around him in a fierce hug. "Well?" she whispered.

"Well, how about letting me get inside to sit down, beautiful?" he said lightly. But his tone was too deliberate. Julie could feel him measuring out his words.

"Please, Matt," she implored. Matt was too controlled. If it were good news, he would have spilled it the second he saw her. She felt sick with fear as she followed him up the stairs and into the living room.

Her eyes were fixed on Matt as he took off his jacket, draped it over the arm of the sofa, and sat down. He held out his hand. She took it, letting him pull her down next to him. Matt squeezed her hand tightly as she settled into the cushions. He looked at her. Deep-set gaze. Serious gaze. Julie needed to know, but suddenly she wanted to stop his words.

"It's Hodgkin's disease," he said quietly.

Julie's feelings were suspended on a current of shock. "Hodgkin's?" she heard herself repeat dully.

"Cancer," Matt said, without displaying any emotion himself. Julie had heard the word in her mind over and over in the past couple of weeks, always to a heart-gripping pain and fright. Now it didn't feel real. Now she felt as if she were watching herself from far away. As if she were somebody else, a stranger. She didn't know what to think. Her mind was numb.

But Matt continued to talk, evenly, calmly. "The reason it took so long for them to let me know is because Dr. Zinn was having my test results analyzed by specialists all over the country." He coughed into his hand. "I've got what they refer to as stage three. That means it's not localized. It's spread past my neck, past my lymph nodes."

Julie could barely comprehend what Matt was saying. "I know it sounds horrible, Jules," he told her. "But listen. It's treatable."

Treatable? Julie felt what Matt was saying beginning to take hold. But by letting in a ray of hope, she let in the fear, too. She felt the sting in her throat as the tears formed and welled up. "What does it mean?" she asked. She realized she was clutching at Matt's hand.

"Well, it's pretty scary, actually. It means I'm going to need intensive radiation and chemotherapy."

Julie had heard those words before. Now it occurred to her that she didn't exactly know what they meant. But instead of asking, she just nodded her head. She needed to hear the rest of it, had to hear all of it, before she started asking questions.

"The treatment's two weeks in the hospital, two weeks out, till I beat this thing," Matt said.

That was it. *That* was what Julie wanted to hear. "But you can," she said. "You *can* beat it."

Matt inclined his head in a kind of half-nod. "I can beat it. *We* can beat it, Jules. The chances are real good."

Chances? But that meant there was a chance for bad, too! "Oh, Matt," Julie whispered. She could feel her body shaking out of control.

Matt grabbed on to her other hand. "Julie, if anyone can lick this, we can. Dr. Zinn said the right attitude is half the battle."

Julie looked into Matt's eyes. He held her gaze. Deep-set gray eyes with rims of green. The gaze she knew so well. She didn't see any sickness there. Or fear. She saw love, Matt's love for her. She felt her own love, felt her soul open wordlessly to his.

And then he smiled. Matt actually smiled.

"Hey, think of it like this incredibly high mountain that I've got to climb. I've got to, so I do, and that's all there is to it," Matt said. Was that a note of giddiness Julie thought she heard in his voice? It was as if he almost relished the challenge.

Julie felt a tidal wave of love and admiration for Matt. Climbing a mountain. "Matt Collins, you would choose to see it that way." She pulled him toward her and wrapped her arms around him. "I'll be with you every step of the way," she said, hoping her words sounded as sure as his. Fear was beating in her heart, but she willed herself to hold it in.

Matt took her face in his hands. "Julie, I love you so much," he said. His voice was fierce with intensity.

"And I love you." Julie stopped the threatening flow of tears by pressing her mouth hard to Matt's. He responded instantly, deeply. Their lips were hungry, their tongues hot, their breaths urgent.

Julie felt all the emotion channeled to their kiss. She grasped at his hair, he hugged her to him as if she might vanish any second. She kissed his eyes, his cheeks, every part of his face. He buried his lips in the curve of her neck, breathing her in greedily. She slid a hand under his shirt, exploring every swell of muscle, every line of bone as if it were new to her.

His fingers played her body with equal intensity. She felt them slipping to the floor, clinging together. They undressed without letting each other go for a second.

They made love uncovered and unprotected, except by the heat of each other's bodies. They made love as if it were the first time and the last time. As if it were the only time. As if there were no moment before and no moment after.

"Cancer." There was a long pause. Matt gripped the phone receiver tightly, waiting for a response. "Dad?"

After another painful moment of silence, his father finally managed a few words. "What—what are you saying? What do you mean, cancer? Are you sure?"

Matt tried to explain what he'd gone through in the past two weeks, but it all came out in a jumble of jittery half-sentences. He could sense his father's stunned reaction on the other line. Telling his dad was turning out to be even harder than he'd thought. "Dr. Zinn said that by combining heavy doses of radiation and chemotherapy, it should—"

"Matt, slow down," his father interrupted. "This is very hard for me to digest. Chemotherapy? That sounds so drastic."

Matt swallowed hard. "Yeah. But it's the best way, Dad."

"Don't you think that maybe you're moving a little too fast on this?"

"The sooner the better," Matt informed him. "Dr. Zinn said my chances are that much better if we start right away."

"Son," Mr. Collins said slowly, as if allowing himself time to take it all in, "I think it would be a good idea if I gave Dr. Lynnstrohm a call and we set up an appointment. I'll wire you the money for a plane ticket."

"Dad, I've got Hodgkin's disease."

"Well, who is this Zinn, anyway?" his father said, his voice beginning to rise. "Shouldn't you at least have a second opinion?"

Matt felt his own frustration beginning to take hold. "Dr. Zinn is a really great doctor. And I've had lots of opinions. He sent my test results all over the country to get analyzed. Dad, Dr. Lynnstrohm was my pediatrician. What's he going to do about cancer?" *Cancer.* The frightening word hung in the air.

There was another long pause. Matt could picture his dad on the other end, running a nervous hand through his thick, wavy hair. He was sitting on a stool at the kitchen counter, no doubt, his knees pressed tightly together, his body hunched over the way it always did when he got upset. Matt realized he was in exactly the same position.

He took a deep breath and tried to exhale

some of the tension. "Look, Dad, I'm not going to die, okay? I promise you. It's not going to happen to *me*. The whole point is that I get it treated now, so that I'll get healthy fast."

"Well, why not come home for the treatment? We'll find a great clinic here in Philly. I haven't touched your old room since you left it."

"Thanks, but just the same, I think I'll stay here, Dad."

"Matt, I'm only thinking of what's best for you," he said. "If chemotherapy is all that people say it is, wouldn't you rather be home for it?"

Matt let out a short laugh that gave way to a coughing spurt. "Dad, I am home. This is where I live. Right here, with Julie."

Another long silence. Very long and very painful. Matt felt almost guilty. He could tell how shocked his father was, how much he was hurting. But Matt's place was here. He was married, an adult, and it was time his father knew it.

"Well . . ." his father finally said. "Have you called your mother yet?"

Matt felt a jolt of disbelief. "My mother?"

"Matt—"

"Forget it, Dad. What would she say? 'Matt? Matt who? Oh, right, the kid I left twelve years ago when I just couldn't cope. The kid I barely ever talk to. Oh, cancer? Gee, that's too bad.'"

His father's voice turned suddenly edgy. "That's enough, son. I don't like what your mother did any more than you do. But—"

"I'll handle this the way I need to, all right?" Matt's tone was harsher than he'd meant it to be. "Look, I'm a big boy, Dad," he said more softly. "Please. I can take care of myself. You've got to believe me."

His father let out an audible sigh. "You always have, son. Hey, I don't suppose you'd want me out there, would you? I mean, if you won't come home. All you have to do is say the word."

"I'm going to be fine, Dad," Matt insisted. He realized he was saying it as much for his own ears as his father's. "No, don't come out. Thanks for the offer, but there wouldn't be anything for you to do out here. I'll keep in touch."

There was a long pause. "Hey, Matt?" his dad said.

"Yeah?"

"I—I love you, Matt, that's all." Another pause. Matt could hear his father sniffling. "Just promise me you'll call if you need anything. And take care of yourself, huh? You're my only son."

Matt felt the emotion building, the tears beginning to well up inside. "I will, Dad. Bye." He placed the receiver into the cradle and blew out a huge breath of air.

"Hey." Julie's voice was gentle. She came in from the bedroom and sat down on the sofa by his side. She took his hand and gave it a tender kiss. "It's going to be okay, remember?"

Matt shrugged. "I know. I just wish he didn't have to be—to be such a dad. I can't stand being treated like a twelve-year-old. And you know what? He asked if I was going to call my mom. Can you believe it?"

"Shhh." Julie kneaded Matt's palm with her thumb. "He probably just freaked out a little when you told him, you know? Trust me, it's hard to hear that somebody you love has cancer."

"I suppose. But no way am I calling my mom. She'd probably celebrate."

"I doubt it. But do what you need to do," Julie said.

"I will. Zinn says, 'Think positive.' There's no room for unnecessary baggage, you know?" Matt let out another hefty sigh.

"Matt?" Julie asked, her voice soft, cautious. "You didn't ask your father about lending us some money to help pay for the bills?"

Matt shook his head. "I couldn't. I'm sorry, but as soon as he laid the little-kid trip on me, I just couldn't. It would be like admitting to him that I couldn't cope, that I *was* still a child. I was too afraid he'd try to force me to go back to Philly."

He looked at Julie, hoping she'd understand. She smiled, but Matt could see the fear beneath it. He couldn't blame her. He had medical coverage, as a spouse on Julie's student health plan. But there were deductibles, hidden expenses, and some things weren't covered at all. "Jules, let's not worry about the bills, huh? They're not going to turn me away."

"I know," Julie said. "And besides, we've got Club Night coming up on Friday. We could take in a bundle."

Matt squeezed her hand hard. "I like that we part, Julie. I really like that *we* part."

Julie smiled. Yes, she was scared, but there was hope mixed in there, too. "Positive thinking, remember?"

Seven

Julie sat across from Dahlia in the corner booth of the campus snack bar, sinking down and trying to make herself as unnoticeable as possible. Trying and failing. As she took a sip of her orange soda, she saw John Graham from her journalism class passing through on his way to the mail room, his long red-blond hair like a beacon in the crowd of students. Mark looked around the snack bar, spotted Julie, and raised his hand in a tentative greeting. On his face was a pained, sorry smile, as if Julie were a lost puppy. Yeah, he knew.

Julie gave a little wave back. "Wow, it seems like everyone on campus and their brother already knows about Matt," she said to Dahlia. "I mean, *we* just found out a couple of days ago. What—did they broadcast it over WMAD or something? Newly Married Freshwoman's Husband Fights Deadly Disease!"

Dahlia shook her head sympathetically. "Campus grapevine. I felt that way at the beginning of the year when those two stooges dumped me on the same day, and Paul said there were all those rumors going around about me. I mean, not that it compares to your situation, but I know what it's like when you think everyone's talking about you. It probably seems worse than it is."

Julie swirled a french fry around in the little paper dish of ketchup, but she didn't eat it. She hadn't had any appetite since she'd found out the bad news. "I don't know, Dahlia. Yesterday at work, it was like, 'Any string beans left? Oh, my God, aren't you the one whose husband—oh, it's so awful.' Or, 'Thanks for the corn, hey, I'm really sorry to hear about—' I mean, they don't even know his name!" She laughed darkly. "And then there are the others who won't look at you at all. Matt's boss, Jake, is like that with him, and half the kids in my classes are, too."

Dahlia let out a long breath. "It stinks, but face it—it *is* kind of impossible to know what to say. I mean, I've never known anyone our age who—" She snapped her mouth shut, as if she were about to make a terrible mistake.

"Say it," Julie said, feeling an awful tightness

inside her chest. "There's a chance that Matt could die." She saw Dahlia grimace, as if the ugly word had stung her. She shrugged. "Most of the time it seems so unreal it doesn't mean anything—like if you say the same word over and over and it stops making sense. Other times—" Julie swallowed hard. "I'm so scared I can't think straight. What's going on with Matt gets all confused in my head with what happened to my sister, and I can't help thinking what if Matt's next?"

"You can't look at it like that, Julie."

Julie leaned back in the booth. At the table across from them, a trio of kids were turning a hot dog into Mr. Potato Head, sticking in toothpicks for arms and legs, crowning it with onion rings for hair, and laughing hysterically as if it were the funniest thing in the world.

"That's the weirdest thing," she said to Dahlia, watching one of the guys take a squirt bottle of mustard and make a face at the end of the hot dog. "Life's just going on as usual for everyone else. I feel like time should stop, or everyone should look different, or something. You know, because *I* feel so different."

"Yeah," Dahlia said softly. She took a sip of coffee. "You know we're all rooting for you guys."

Julie nodded.

"Marion, Susan, everyone on the hall . . .

Nick asked about Matt in class the other day. He's really concerned about him."

"I know. I bumped into him when I was leaving the library last night," Julie said.

"Lucky you," Dahlia said with a sheepish smile.

Julie gave a little laugh. "I guess we're getting to be friends again. Sort of. I mean, as much as we can, considering I'm afraid to mention his name around Matt. Not that I can blame him."

Dahlia drained her coffee cup. "Hey, it's over," she said. "You can't feel guilty for the rest of your life over a few kisses. It happens. Well, to some fortunate people."

Julie felt a bubble of real laughter. "Sussman, you're hopeless. Since when did you ever think you couldn't get the guy?"

Dahlia pouted. "Since Nick Stone, is when. He's totally cute, but he's immune to my many charms," she cracked sourly.

"What about that class?" Julie asked. "You know—good art, a dark room, Italian things. It was supposed to be about as romantic as school got."

Dahlia blew out a noisy breath. "Well, I got another word wrong yesterday. There's a way of laying the paint on really thick—it's called *impasto,* except that I called it *impasta.* Nick's sitting right next to me. Or actually, I'm sitting next to him—I did the sitting, of course—and he goes, im*pasta*? With tomato sauce or Alfredo?"

Julie giggled.

"Go ahead and laugh. Everybody else did," Dahlia said. "I'm sure he thinks I'm a total moron in addition to being a spoiled brat."

"Dahlia, I think the guy was joking around with you. If he hated you, I really don't think he'd bother."

"You don't? Every time I think there's a chance with him, I end up fooling myself. I'm not sure he'd even talk to me if he didn't want to find out about Matt."

Matt. Julie felt herself tighten up again. Dahlia must have read her expression, because she reached across the table and grabbed Julie's hand. "Listen, you've got to believe he's going to be okay. The doctors say he's got a real good chance, right?"

"Right."

"And his head's in the right place."

That was the truth. Right this moment Matt was out somewhere on his mountain bike, pedaling away. "Strength is the key to it all," he'd said confidently this morning, as he was bundling up to go out. If it weren't for his cough, and those darned lab tests, you wouldn't even know he was sick.

"Yeah, Matt's actually dealing with this better than any of us," Julie said. "I guess I've just got to try to stay as up as he is."

"Well, any time you want some company," Dahlia said, "I'm more than psyched to get away from Cindi-i-i-i."

Julie raised an eyebrow. "Now what?" She felt a twinge of guilt for being secretly glad that Cindi was getting on Dahlia's nerves. She knew she would have been jealous if Dahlia's new roommate had become her new best friend. "So what did she do now?" Julie asked.

"Nothing new. Just the same as always," Dahlia said. "'Dahlia, I found this new, all-natural face scrub with sea minerals,'" Dahlia said extra brightly. "'You can use it if you want. Gee, did you see Sarah's new haircut? Doesn't it look just super on her? It practically makes her aura shimmer. Hey, did I tell you about the breathing group some people are starting over at Harper House?'" Dahlia shook her head. "Oh, and did I tell you she has succeeded in getting me to do yoga with her first thing in the morning?"

Julie laughed. Dahlia wasn't exactly a morning person.

"I had to give in. She just wouldn't leave me alone."

"Well, you've got an invitation to come over any time she gets to you," Julie said. She had a feeling her little apartment might suddenly seem too big with Matt in the hospital. A cramp of fear took hold of her.

"I'll be there," Dahlia said. "I promise."

A few days later, Julie trudged across the Green and down Main Street, her step heavy. The sky was gray and flat, the air bitter. She could barely remember anything about the past few hours. She'd gone to morning classes and worked the lunch shift, but her mind was in a fog. She was afraid to think or feel. She walked mechanically, numbly.

This was the last day. Tomorrow, Matt went into the hospital. Julie passed Books and Things without even glancing in the window. Matt kept talking about how in two weeks he would be home again. Like he was going on a little vacation, and when he came back everything would be just as it had been. But then there would be another two weeks of treatment the next month, and the next. And the break from the hospital and the chemotherapy—Dr. Zinn had explained to Matt that it was so his body could recover between treatments. In killing the cancer cells, healthy cells were destroyed, too.

Julie shuddered. That meant that Matt was going to come home from the hospital feeling worse than when he'd gone in. She shifted her shoulder bag forward and felt around absently in the front zipper pocket for her house keys. Her hand found the knob of polished redwood that hung from her key chain, a present from Matt when he and his old high-school buddy, Steven, had gone out to California last year on Christmas vacation.

"For good luck," Matt had said. Julie rubbed the wood with her fingers. *As if it's really going to cure Matt.* She unlocked the downstairs door and pushed it open.

She heard it immediately. The sound of laughter. Matt's laugh, raucous and strong, and someone else's, too. Julie felt a jolt of surprise. Matt was checking into the cancer ward of Great Lakes Hospital in the morning, and he was upstairs laughing!

"When you're all better, we'll put you on the Olympic swim team." Julie recognized Leon's voice coming down the stairs.

"Oh, man! Like a baby's behind. Smooth!" she heard Matt respond, breaking into hysterical laughter.

Julie rushed upstairs. What was going on in there? She fumbled with her keys, trying to get the door open fast. As the lock clicked, the laughter inside stopped.

"Dum-de-dum-dum!" Leon sang, in his velvet tenor. Julie saw Leon coming out of the bathroom toward her, trying to hold back a funny little grin. "Hey, Julie," he greeted her.

"Don't blame me. It was his idea. See you, Matt," he called out over his shoulder, edging past her to the door.

And before she could say hello or good-bye to Leon, Matt was emerging from the bathroom, too. "Thanks, Leon," he yelled as Leon clattered down the stairs. "I appreciate your help."

Julie felt an involuntary catch of breath. She knew her mouth was hanging open, her eyes huge. Matt stood in the living room in a pair of worn jeans, his upper torso bare—and his head as smooth and hairless as an egg. He was totally bald!

"Oh, my God!" Julie exclaimed.

Matt grinned. "Shocking, I know. But what do you think?"

Matt's eyebrows stood out thick and decisive, the only dark color left on his face. His features looked stronger, more noticeable—his straight, broad nose and full lips somehow more defined. Even the faint scar on the inside corner of his eye and the freckle near his mouth were more prominent.

"Why?" Julie managed.

Matt gave a half-cough, half-laugh, and shrugged. "Well, you know what they say about the effects of the chemo. I figured if my hair's going to fall out, I wanted to be the one to get rid of it. You know, take matters into my own hands. Besides, I figure it'll look tough with my motorcycle."

Julie understood what Matt was telling her without saying it right out. He was going to conquer the disease before it conquered him. She pulled her mouth into a smile. "You're beautiful. With or without," she said. She reached toward his gleaming scalp. "Now come here so I can touch it."

Matt came over and lowered his head dutifully. Julie put a tentative hand on it. The top of his head was almost totally round, with a slight bulge at the back. His skin felt incredibly soft over the firmness of his skull. She started giggling. "It's so smooth!"

Matt laughed, too. "Well, now we know how I'll look when I'm old." He wrapped his arms around her and kissed her on the cheek.

Julie felt her laughter freeze in her throat. *If* he grew old. With Matt all shaved and prepared to do battle with huge machines and a hospital full of drugs, she couldn't help feeling that the clock was ticking faster than ever.

"Just hold me, Matt," she said.

Matt squeezed her harder. "I'm going to beat it, Jules," he said. "Just believe in me."

Eight

Matt sat in a cushioned, wooden armchair in the cancer-ward waiting room. Rather than the usual drab green walls and dingy fluorescent fixtures of the rest of the hospital, this room had a fresh coat of canary-yellow paint and modern track lighting. Sunlight poured in through a bank of floor-to-ceiling windows, warming him in his skimpy hospital gown. Except for the slight smell of disinfectant, it was okay. Definitely a lot more comfortable than Matt had expected it would be.

He'd already done his early-morning radiation treatment, and now chemotherapy awaited him. So far, not so awful. The radiation had lasted about an hour. Basically, an hour of boredom—sequestered away in a lead-walled room, his body covered with heavy lead sheets, it didn't feel too different than when he'd had the intensive X rays taken a few weeks ago. The technician would come in every few minutes, smile, adjust the lead pads, and get as far away as possible before turning on the machine. A little red light would go on every time the radiation was pumping into him. It sort of felt like being in an old sci-fi movie. Matt wondered how long it would take till he'd be glowing like a nuclear power plant after a meltdown. Chalk it all up to the amazing world of advanced medicine. But if it was going to make him better—and he was certain it would—then turn up the volume. He could deal with it.

Part two, the chemo treatment, was the frightening part. Through the double doors to the treatment rooms that swung open every minute or so, Matt caught petrifying glimpses of other patients struggling through it. Some were lying down, their bodies wriggling with pain. Others sat up in their beds, wincing, moaning, crying. He saw a young man who looked to be about his own age violently vomiting into a bedpan, holding on for dear life to the metal pole that his I.V. bag was hooked on to. The weird orange liquid—the stuff Matt was told was going to make him sick—oozed out of the bags into each patient's veins. Martianlike nurses buzzed around the room wearing green smocks, green face masks, and green rubber gloves, while they monitored the patients and their liquids.

The worst part of it all was that he was alone. Julie had wanted to come out with him today. She was going to skip a few classes and bring her work with her. But Matt had insisted she stay home. "Life goes on." He'd reminded her over and over again of the philosophy he'd come to base his recovery on. The whole point of it was to keep on going. Keep on living without fear. No need to change the day-to-day—it would only be admitting defeat. That's the attitude it took to beat the disease. But sitting there now, his stomach hollow with fright, Matt wished that just this once he'd been a little less macho and let Julie come along. Holding her hand now would have made things seem a lot more hopeful.

"Don't worry," a high-pitched, squeaky voice said. "It's not as bad as it looks."

A little boy was sitting next to Matt. From the size of him, he looked to be about seven years old. But dressed in the same drab gray hospital gown as Matt, his fuzzy, blue-white head, his puffy, bloated cheeks, and his frail body made him look like an old man. Matt was taken, though, by the cheek-to-cheek smile on the boy's face.

"It's my first time," Matt said to him.

"Yeah, I figured. Think of it like this—it's

going to hurt a little, but when it's over, you're that much closer to getting better." The boy gave Matt a funny little wave. "I'm Danny. Danny O'Brien."

"Hi, Danny. I'm Matt Collins. Nice to meet you."

Danny instantly got excited. "Matt Collins? Really? You and I are going to be roommates for the next few weeks. All right!" he cheered, suddenly seeming very much like a little boy, despite the aged appearance.

Matt laughed. "Hey, what are you, a private eye or something? How do you know we're going to be roommates?"

"I checked into my room already and saw your charts by your bed. I wanted to drop off some of my things before my treatment. You know, baseball cards, candy, stuff like that."

"Well, I bet we'll make excellent roommates," Matt said. "If you've got to be stuck in here, might as well be stuck with someone fun, right?"

"Definitely. Not like the last few months. Mr. Harper, he was about a hundred years old. Moaned all the time. Never smiled. Never wanted to watch games on TV, either."

"What happened to him?" Matt asked.

Danny shrugged, his smile disappearing momentarily. But then it resurfaced. "Anyway, it's really not too bad around here. The food sort of stinks, but you get used to it. The nurses are real nice, except for Mrs. Rodriguez."

"Yeah, I've noticed," Matt said.

"Like last night, I was reading about Babe Ruth's first World Series game. Right when he was stepping up to the plate, *bam!*—Mrs. Rodriguez shuts my lights off." Danny slammed his hand on his knee. Matt could tell the boy had spunk. "Anyway, don't worry about the chemo," he said, pointing to the swinging door. "Yeah, it'll hurt. But it's worth it."

"You seem pretty tough," Matt said.

Danny shrugged. "I guess. I just want to get better. I've got plans for the future, you know?"

Matt listened to Danny go on about how when he beat leukemia he could go back to playing Little League baseball. And eventually, the little boy would be pitching for the Chicago Cubs. Danny was filled with hope and dreams of the future. Just as Matt was. Matt felt a well of courage.

Until Danny told Matt that he was ten years old. Ten, not seven, as Matt had thought. And that he'd been in treatment for two years! He was extremely weak and undersized. Danny's doctor had originally told him he'd need only six months of treatment. Matt felt his optimism draining away. Was he himself only at the beginning of the kind of uphill battle that Danny had been fighting for a major portion of his life?

The door swung open again, and a nurse approached them. Matt watched Danny's face turn frighteningly pale, his body tighten with fear.

"Danny, honey. Your turn," a green-gowned nurse said, offering a sympathetic hand to the boy, easing him up from his chair.

Matt felt his own panic building as he watched Danny walk away. How bad could it be? Matt swore to himself that he'd beat it—the pain, the extra months of treatment, everything. He was different. He was stronger than the others, wasn't he?

But as he looked around, he wondered if it was so easy. Sure, the waiting room had cheerful yellow walls, and big framed paintings of flower gardens and beaches. But the dozen or so people in the waiting room all had cancer. Some of them were completely bald, others wore wigs, hiding the effects of the treatment. Everyone looked weak and tired and scared. Who here was going to make it out alive?

I love you, Matt. He remembered Julie's parting words and good-bye kiss before he'd hopped on his bike and ridden out here this morning. The feel of her arms around his waist. Her sweet, fresh scent, her soft, full lips. "I love you the most," she'd said. Matt wished again that she could be here now.

Matt closed his eyes and made himself a promise that nothing was going to get in the way of his recovery—nothing. If anyone was going to beat cancer, he was. And fast.

"Matt Collins?" a voice called out. He opened his eyes to a smiling, Martian-green nurse holding a clipboard and motioning in the direction of that horrible room.

Julie sat at the edge of Matt's empty, starched white hospital bed. The door to the bathroom was closed, but that didn't stop her from hearing the horrible sounds. Matt's stomach-wrenching moans were punctuated only by his episodes of violent vomiting. Julie didn't know how there was anything left inside him. It sounded as if he must be throwing up every organ, every bit of blood and gut. Julie had a sour taste at the back of her mouth, a rotten taste. It sounded as if Matt's very soul were being wrenched loose.

She pressed her fingers in her ears, but she couldn't block out the sounds. Should she go help him? But help him do what? She couldn't bear to see him this way. She felt paralyzed, unable to move from his bed.

In the next bed over, Danny lay with his eyes closed. Julie couldn't believe he could sleep through this. On the other hand, he'd gone through the same thing not too long before. With every ounce of strength pried out of you, what else could you do but lie down and pass out, cold and spent? Only a few sparse, pale hairs clung to Danny's scalp, and his face, just a child's face, was so puffy it was hard to tell what he must have looked like before he'd gotten sick. He was so young. It seemed so unfair.

Julie couldn't help thinking of her brother, Tommy, who was just a little older than Danny. She glanced at the Cubs pennant over Danny's bed. Like Danny, Tommy was a big baseball fan. They both liked mysteries and video games. They both thought Matt was Mr. Cool. Would they have been friends if they'd met in the school yard, or out on a ball field? Julie felt a wave of longing to see her brother. She missed him so much. And the rest of her family, too.

The hospital seemed to infect her with its sickness and sadness. How many times, in the few hours she'd been here, had she found herself thinking about Mary Beth? Or the fact that her parents felt so out of reach?

Two weeks of this. Two awful weeks. Julie didn't know how she could come out here every day and see Matt like this. Two weeks, and then a brief reprieve. And then more of the same, again. Julie shuddered.

From the other side of the bathroom door,

Matt's groans weakened, giving way to moments of silence. A long sigh, full of relief. Julie heard the toilet flush, the water in the shower go on. Finally. Finally. A few minutes later the door opened, and Matt stood there, wet, a towel wrapped around him.

Julie forced a smile. He looked extremely pale. His eyes were dull. But he managed a tiny smile back. "I think it's over," he said weakly.

But Julie knew it was far from over. She knew that this was only the beginning.

Nine

The apartment was spick-and-span. The floor was vacuumed, the furniture polished. Every appliance in the kitchen shone. On the table was a chocolate-raspberry cake with chocolate frosting—a little lopsided, but Julie had baked it herself. On the top, in red icing, she'd written, "Welcome home, Matt."

Dressed up in her black silk pants and a beaded vintage sweater from Secondhand Rose, Julie glanced at the kitchen clock for the umpteenth time. She felt a tingling, excited sort of nervousness, like before a big party. Dahlia had offered to drive Julie to the hospital to pick Matt up, but Matt had insisted on getting home on his own steam.

"Two weeks of freedom!" he'd told Julie the other day, triumph in his voice. "No ringing for nurses every time I want to sneeze, no special passes just to take a walk outside."

Julie could picture him on his motorcycle, zooming down the highway toward Madison right now. If she knew Matt, he was probably shouting into the wind at the top of his voice.

Julie sank onto the sofa and waited impatiently. It had been the most difficult two weeks of her life, except perhaps for the first two after Mary Beth had died. Two weeks of racing from class to work to the hospital and back again. Two weeks of presenting Matt with her most cheerful face, bringing him comedy videos so they could laugh together—laughing as if there weren't a thing wrong—only to return home and burst into tears when no one was looking.

Dahlia had been wonderful, shuttling Julie back and forth most days, and even trying to teach her to drive a stick so she could take the little red sports car out to visit Matt by herself. But Julie was too keyed up to get the shifting down. Last weekend, she'd stalled out on the corner of Main and Cherry, with several cars behind her, honking like furious geese.

"Yo, is that how they teach you to drive in college?" the guy in the pickup truck in back of her had yelled out his window. Julie had sat there at the green light, tears of frustration running down her cheeks, until Dahlia had switched seats with her and gotten the car going again.

But the two weeks would have been even harder if Matt's mood had been as bad as his health. Instead, he'd stayed positive and upbeat, certain his battle against cancer was being won.

The familiar sound of Matt's bike had Julie up and out of her seat and flying down the stairs. The sting of cold air hit her as she raced outside without a coat.

"Jules! You're going to freeze!" Matt threw his arms around her. Julie hugged him back, holding on with all her might. Even with his leather jacket on, she could feel how thin he'd gotten during his stay at the hospital, and when she finally let go and looked up into his face, it was puffy and pale. As he removed his helmet, she could see his bald head was wrapped in a red bandanna, giving him the look of a seasick pirate. But he was smiling at her, his eyes full of life.

"Brrr. Maybe you're not cold, but I am," he said between kisses. "Think we can continue this inside?"

Julie nodded, stooping down to reach for the small duffel bag Matt had brought home from the hospital with him. But Matt got to it first, grabbing it with one hand, without letting Julie go with the other.

In the living room, he dropped the bag in the middle of the floor and shed his jacket. "Home from the wars," he said. "Man, does it feel good." Then he wrapped his arms around her again.

The cake could wait. Julie felt the weeks of tension giving way under Matt's touch. Maybe she'd never quite let herself believe that she and Matt would be standing here again, hugging as they had so many times before. Maybe, she thought, as she let her muscles relax, her breath deepen, she'd been preparing for the worst without even realizing it.

But that didn't matter now. All that counted was the feel of Matt's body next to hers, his hands running gently up and down her back, his lips on her neck, her cheek, her brow. His lips on her lips. He took her by the hand and led her into the bedroom.

They undressed each other slowly. Julie felt Matt's gaze. It never left her. But she lowered her eyes from his overly lean torso, the ribs and muscles standing out more than usual. After two weeks alone, she felt almost shy.

They lay down on the bed and exchanged a few soft, gentle kisses. Julie felt her shyness melting away in the warm familiarity of Matt's embrace. She traced the features she knew so well—the straight, broad nose, the full lips. She kissed his eyes. He smiled and kissed her back.

Their kisses deepened.

But as Julie began to lose herself in the slow, heightened sensations of their bodies, Matt rolled away from her. The spell was broken. "Matt?"

Matt turned back toward her and reached out his hand. He caressed her shoulder and ran his finger across her collarbone. He came closer and kissed her again. But there was a hesitancy to it. He stopped once more.

"Is something wrong?" Julie asked. Was Matt feeling shy, too?

"It's not going to work," Matt said, embarrassed. "They told me this might happen after the chemo." He flopped onto his back and stared up at the ceiling, his lips pressed together.

Julie felt her heart go out to him. Matt was trying so hard to act as though everything were normal. But everything was not normal. She put a hand on his arm. His body was strung tight. "Matt," she said softly. "Hey, it's okay." She moved closer to him.

"I'm sorry," Matt muttered.

Julie put her arms around him. "There's nothing to be sorry about. I just want you here. I just need to hold you—and you to hold me." Matt was stiff in her embrace. "Please," she whispered, not letting him go.

After a while his body began to give way, to

relax. He shifted slightly, molding himself to her hug. "I don't want to let go, either," he whispered. "I love you. So much."

"I love you, too." Julie hugged him harder.

A hefty gust of raw March wind blew straight into Matt's face as he pedaled his mountain bike furiously uphill through the wooded landscape. He breathed deeply, embracing the wilderness. The tail end of winter with spring trying to break through—it was the perfect weather for his battle with cancer. The wind whistled through the swaying trees, blowing the last bits of a recent snowfall off their near-bare branches. Matt's face was beaded with sweat. Faster and harder, somewhere beyond physical exhaustion lay the road to recovery.

As he braked to a stop at a sharp turn in the trail, Matt looked back. There was no sign at all of Leon, who'd come along for his afternoon workout. When he'd accompanied him a few days ago, Matt had had to wait over half an hour at the end of the trail for Leon to show up, so he decided to hop off his bike and wait for him now.

Matt inhaled and exhaled a few big breaths of air. On each exhale, he focused his mind on blowing the toxins out of his body. Out and away forever. With every exhalation of air, and with each pedal of his bike, each push-up and sit-up, Matt could feel himself getting stronger, and more important, healthier. The bandage from his biopsy was gone, the scar was healing, and the cough that had landed him in the doctor's office in the first place was practically nonexistent.

By the time Leon arrived, panting as usual, Matt was already on his second repetition of fifty push-ups. "Ten more and I finish my daily quota," he said, dipping his chest down to the ground and back up again.

"Hey, Mr. Olympian, I thought you said you had cancer. You might be getting better, but this workout is killing me, man."

Matt laughed. "I always said you were a wimp, Leon. But I still love you. Now look, I lost count."

"You're on about a million," Leon said. "Hey, are you sure your superdoc said this is okay? You've been going at it full steam, all day every day."

Matt sucked in his stomach and did a final ten push-ups. "There. A million, like you said." He rolled over on his back and reached out his arms to grab his left leg, stretching it up toward him to work out the tightness from the biking. "Yeah, it's okay. In fact, Dr. Zinn said that exercise is the best thing for me. If it keeps me happy and strong, go for it. The trick is to keep my white blood cell count up high enough to keep my immune system healthy. Sometimes the chemotherapy can drain it. But as long as my count stays high enough, I can keep up with the exercise."

"Sounds like you know what you're talking about, Matt," Leon said.

"Actually, that's what I like about Dr. Zinn. He doesn't have me resigned to a hospital bed. That's the whole key—not to think sick, you know? It's like this guy I was reading about. He had Hodgkin's, too. My age. He was doing canoe marathons in between chemo treatments. It was pretty amazing. And the best part about it is that he's all better now."

Leon nodded. "Sure. Makes sense to me. All that mind-over-matter stuff. It's the same with the horn. You think you can hit a certain note, and what do you know, you hit it."

"Exactly. I can feel it working. I know I'm getting better fast."

"Well, the last thing you look to me is sick. Seriously, Matt, you seem really great," Leon said, smiling.

"You mean it? Thanks." Matt got up and headed for his bike.

"Uh-oh, the triathlon continues," Leon said with a shrug. "Oh, I almost forgot, Matt. I bumped into your pal Nick the other day in town. He was asking about you. Wanted to know if he could do anything for you."

"My ex-pal, you mean," Matt snapped. The mere mention of his name brought on a giant wave of anger and frustration.

"Still?"

Matt let out a bitter laugh. "If Nick had things his way, I wouldn't survive this thing."

"Don't be ridiculous," Leon scolded. "The guy sounded pretty concerned to me."

"Yeah, well, don't let his act fool you, Leon." Maybe it was a little silly to still be so furious with the guy, but the last thing Matt needed now was any more grief pumping through his system. "Look, let's just forget about it, okay? I'm into only positive thinking these days."

"You got it, boss," Leon said.

Matt smiled. Leon knew where his head was at. "Hey, thanks, Lip. You're okay, man. Really. I mean, everybody else around town is either afraid to look at me and my big bald head, or else they're so overly polite and out-of-the-way helpful it's pathetic. Even Julie's different these days. At first, this was our thing. Our problem, you know? We were going through cancer together. But she's so worried all the time. She tries to hide it, tries to pretend everything's cool, but it's not working. It's like she just doesn't believe I can lick this thing. Anyway, Leon, you're different than everybody else. You seem to understand where I'm at."

"Hey, man, you're choking me up."

"I'm serious," Matt said. "You're just you, like you've always been."

"I wouldn't know who else to be," Leon said matter-of-factly.

"Well, just keep it up, okay?" Matt hopped on his bike. "Now, are we riding or what? I've got another few miles left to blow some more toxins out of my system."

"I'm following."

"I sure didn't think you were leading."

Matt worked his way up to a quick pace. He could hear Leon behind him, starting to fade into the distance. "Hey, Leon!" he shouted back to him. "How about making up a blues song about me. Like this. 'I'm going to sweat out my cancer, baby'—"

"Gimme a break!" Leon called out, his voice getting softer with each pedal Matt took. "Just keep riding," he called out from behind.

Ten

Marion felt Fred's hand wrapped tightly around her waist, pulling her closer. His other hand cupped the back of her head. His lips were searching hers. Everything in its usual place. Same scene, different evening. The only change was the location. Today they stood outside the library, while Fred planted endless kisses on her lips and face. Yesterday it had been the dining hall, the day before that her dorm, the day before that . . .

As she kissed him back, her mind started to wander. The upcoming biology midterm was only a week away, and she still wasn't entirely comfortable with the new material. She and Fred had just spent three hours in the library going over lab notes. Well, that's what they were supposed to be doing. Being lab partners with the guy you were going out with was impossible, though. How could you memorize genetic and embryologic terminology when you were always locked in an embrace?

Marion started going through what she could remember in her head. *Let's see. When two like alleles are inherited from an organism's two parents, then it's homozygous. But what about entelechy? I was just reading about it, but now I don't remember. I should know that. What about oocyte? Oh yeah, that's the female gamete, the one with the haploid number of chromosomes. I think, anyway . . .*

"Marion? Earth to Marion. Earth to Marion."

"Huh?" Marion was startled. Earth to Marion was right. She'd totally forgotten what she was doing.

"You okay, sweetheart?" Fred asked, rubbing the back of her neck.

"Sure," she said. She closed her eyes. Their lips met, and they settled back into their kiss.

But within seconds her thoughts started to wander again. She'd told Susan she'd try to meet her back at their dorm room by nine-thirty so they could go visit Matt and Julie for an hour. Was it nine-thirty already? And she was supposed to call her parents tonight, too, to check in. Two of the cows were about to give birth on the farm, and Marion wanted to see if they'd delivered yet. What would they name them? Marion wanted Zora and Clara if they were females, and Rafael and Felix if they were males.

She heard the sound of a motorcycle in the distance. Marion wondered if it might be Matt. She could picture him whizzing along Main Street. He looked totally cool on his bike in his leather jacket and a pair of faded jeans, and even cooler when he got off the bike and took off his helmet to show off his baby-smooth, round head. Matt was really a great guy. Smart, sweet, fun, adventurous. And great for Julie, too. Marion really hoped his treatment was working.

"Yoo-hoo. Marion? Hello?"

Marion pulled her head back and opened her eyes.

"I—I'm sorry if I startled you. Don't you like my kisses anymore?" Fred asked in a wounded-puppy sort of way.

"Of course I do, Fred." Marion ran her hand through his wavy hair, trying to comfort him.

"But it's like you just disappeared again. What were you thinking about, anyway?"

Marion drew a blank for a second. What was she thinking about? So many things. "Um, I was just wondering about Matt and Julie. You know, how he's doing and all. I guess I'm really worried about him."

Fred took her hand and gave it a tender squeeze. "You're really a good friend, Marion."

Marion couldn't help but feel a twinge of guilt. True, she had been thinking about Matt, but she knew that wasn't why she'd blanked out on Fred. It wasn't right to use Matt's sickness as an excuse. So why was her mind wandering so much? she wondered.

Marion looked up at Fred. He looked back at her with devoted eyes. He was everything a boyfriend should be. Cute, nice, smart, devoted, and a great kisser. But Marion could feel that there was something wrong. Her head was telling her one thing, her heart another. She'd felt it a little bit a few days ago, right here in front of the library, when they'd kissed until practically midnight. And she'd felt it a little again last night, too.

She smiled at Fred. But she saw the doubt that registered in his eyes and his slightly drooping mouth. Fred wasn't convinced.

"Nothing from nothing leaves nothing," Julie muttered to herself. She sat in the kitchen with a pile of bills and her checkbook in front of her. Letting out a sigh, she signed the hospital bill for Matt's first treatment and stuffed it into an envelope. Even with health insurance, the bills piled up faster than she could dream of paying them. Deductibles, hidden extras, special lab fees. And Matt unable to work for two weeks out of every month. Julie dropped the sealed envelope down on the table. She and Matt couldn't even afford to get sick.

She pushed her chair back and tried to stave off the fear and frustration that were becoming all too familiar to her. Matt's attitude was probably the best one: Take it one day at a time. Then again, Matt was out at the gym while Julie took care of the bills—or didn't take care of them—so that he wouldn't have to worry about anything but getting healthy again. That was the important thing. That Matt got better. It was the only thing that mattered.

Julie gave a start at the jangle of the telephone, but she rushed to answer it, glad to get away from the table full of bad news. "Hello?"

"Julie!"

"Mom!" Julie felt a shot of surprise, followed by a vague discomfort. How many weeks had it been since she'd talked to her mother? Weeks. Maybe as much as a month. The last time was definitely before Matt's diagnosis—or simply "Before," as Julie had taken to thinking of it.

"I've been trying to call you for days!" her mother said.

Julie went even more tense. What was wrong? Why the urgency in her voice? "We've been out a lot," she said, her next breath hanging on her mother's response. Why was she calling?

"Honey . . . Why didn't you tell us?" Concern and hurt mingled in her mother's voice.

"Oh," Julie said. The single syllable hung in the air. There was a drawn-out silence. "How—? How did you find out?"

Julie's mother let out a tired breath. "Jerry Collins came into Saint George's this morning."

Julie gave a start. Matt's father? In her father's church? Mr. Collins wasn't a churchgoer. He wasn't even religious. "To talk to Dad?" Julie asked.

"Well, perhaps that wasn't his intention when he came in. I think he was just looking for a little—" She paused, hunting around for the right word. "Comfort," she said. "He was sitting by himself in one of the pews in the front of the church. His head was bowed. Needless to say, your father was surprised to see him—and even more surprised to see him praying. I don't think your father planned on saying anything to Jerry Collins. I expect his presence made your father rather uncomfortable."

I expect so, Julie thought to herself, her mouth setting in a grim line. There was no love lost between her parents and Matt's dad.

"But when Jerry looked up, your father saw the tears on his cheeks," her mother said quietly.

The thought of Jerry Collins crying was something Julie had never pictured, something she could barely imagine. Hearing about it touched something deep inside her. Why, Matt's dad was in the same kind of pain Julie was. Yes, of course he must be. Yet this was the first time she had stopped to think about it. Matt's tough, self-sufficient father, the onetime race-car driver who wasn't afraid of anything, had something to be afraid of now.

At least Julie had Matt to hold on to, to hug and talk to—to feel him alive—alive and with her. Sure, Matt's dad always seemed to have some girlfriend or other, some flavor of the month, but it wasn't real love. When you got right down to it, Julie thought, Matt's dad was all alone, struggling with his pain. "So what did Dad do?" she asked her mother.

"Well, it was only proper for him to go over and offer a few words of support—as the reverend of the church should."

"And he told Dad about Matt," Julie said.

"Honey, why didn't you tell us right away?" her mother asked again.

Julie shrugged. "I know how you feel about Matt," she said. There was a long, uncomfortable pause.

"You know, Julie, your father and I don't agree with some of the choices you've made. But whatever you do, you're our daughter and we love you and want only happiness for you."

Julie swallowed, her throat tight. After hardening herself to the trouble between herself and her parents, she wasn't prepared for the way her mom's tender words cut right to her heart. Even before she and Matt had eloped, her parents didn't often put their affection into words.

"Mom, I—I love you, too," Julie said, blinking away the tears before they could form. "I'm glad Dad said something to Mr. Collins."

Her mother sighed. "I only hope it offered some little drop of solace. We—we know, of course—" Her voice grew strained and she was having trouble putting her thoughts into words. "We know what it's like to—lose a child."

Julie's throat stung. "Mom, Matt's not dead!" *Yet,* she thought, the unwanted word forcing itself into her mind.

"No, no, of course not," her mother said immediately. "It's just that—Julie, your father and I can feel for Jerry Collins. Whatever we may think of him otherwise."

Now Julie was helpless against her tears. She hadn't heard Mom open up this way since before her sister's death. She trembled silently, her cheeks wet.

"Julie?"

"Hmm? Yeah," Julie managed to say through her tears.

"We miss you. Your father and Tommy and I—we all do. If there's anything we can do—anything—you let us know."

"Thanks, Mom." Julie wiped at her cheeks with the back of her hand. "Mom?"

"Sweetheart?"

"Does Tommy know?" Tommy thought Matt was the coolest guy on two wheels.

"We thought it might be better not to tell him. Not just now."

"Well . . . maybe you won't have to," Julie said, hoping with every nerve in her body it would be true.

"Maybe we won't," her mother said. "Now, remember, if you need us . . ."

"I'll remember."

"Good-bye, honey."

"Bye, Mom." Julie waited until she heard the click on her mother's end. As soon as she hung up, the tears started up again fresh. This time, she didn't hold back her sobs.

Eleven

Chiaroscuro, impasto, intonaco. The list of words and phrases that had been so totally foreign to Dahlia at the beginning of the semester was sinking in now. More than sinking in. As Professor Godarotti flicked the lights on after another in-depth slide lecture about the Sistine Chapel, three things came into view. Three items lay testament to the fact that anything was possible.

First, on Dahlia's desk, was her notebook, filled with information from today's lecture. She'd scribbled furiously all through class, putting the professor's views into her own words.

Second, was the paper that Dahlia had written, lying on the desk next to her notebook. Ms. Godarotti had handed it back at the beginning of class: "Me and Michelangelo—Seeing

Isn't Always Believing." The cover page of the essay she'd struggled over was adorned with a giant red A. "Excellent—*Molto bene*" was penned underneath, followed by an in-depth criticism from her teacher.

The third thing Dahlia noticed as her eyes readjusted to the light was Nick. He was looking at her—and he was smiling. Indeed, anything *was* possible.

"Maybe you'll write the next paper for me," he said to her as he gathered up his books. Nick's paper wasn't as proudly displayed as Dahlia's, but then again, Nick wasn't the one trying to prove something. Dahlia had made sure to leave her essay right out in plain view. And it had paid off.

"Beginner's luck, I guess." She couldn't wipe the proud smile off her face. "Maybe she's an easier grader than I thought."

"I doubt it, judging from most of the other kids' reactions when they got theirs back," Nick said. "I think there were a lot of disappointed junior art historians in class today."

Dahlia laughed. "Yeah, did you see that one girl who burst into tears? Total freak-out. I thought I'd be like her when I got mine back. I don't know, maybe sitting next to you is starting to rub off," she said flirtatiously.

"Well, I wouldn't advise you to sit anywhere near me in calculus. Unless you want to flunk out," he said. Not quite the response she'd hoped for, but maybe that was Nick's style of humor. He was still smiling, anyway.

Dahlia stuffed her books into her leather bag and headed out of the classroom with him. The A was one thing. She *had* worked hard on the paper, harder than she'd ever worked on a school assignment. And she'd actually found it fascinating, too. But even better, Nick was walking with her, paying attention to her. The last time together, they'd broken the ice. Today, Dahlia was determined to move way beyond that.

She tried to plot a strategy. She figured that Nick was heading to the mail room and then to lunch. Should she ask him to eat with her, or let him do the asking? The voice inside her said: *Wait. Don't push your luck.* But she was tempted to ignore the voice and just ask him anyway.

As they walked across Central Bowl, Dahlia played down the waves from three different guys as best she could. One of them, Max from her English class, looked a little stung by her unemotional "hi." Max was cute, and fun to flirt with, but he wasn't her type, and Dahlia wasn't about to let anything spoil her chances with Nick.

"Well, congratulations again," Nick said as he pushed open the door to the mail room.

"Even though you know I don't agree with you about the chapel." Nick was a total advocate for any archaeological undertaking—uncover and discover. Dahlia, the "romantic," as Nick had referred to her before, liked the ceiling just the way it was—dark and mysterious.

Lunch. What about lunch? Dahlia wondered.

"Oh, hey," Nick said, turning back toward her. A serious, slightly nervous look appeared on his face, the kind she'd seen countless times when guys were about to ask her out. "Any news about Matt?" he asked.

Dahlia's smile drooped into a disappointed frown. This was a scene that had repeated itself way too many times. Nick got her hopes up, only to end up interested in Matt and Julie, and not her. "He's fine," she said.

Worry filled Nick's eyes. "You sure? You sound like there might be a problem or something."

Problem, yes. But it's not what you think. Dahlia could see that Nick's concern over Matt was deep and totally genuine. The guy was filled with sensitivity and caring. Here Nick was, worrying himself sick over Matt, when Matt couldn't even stand the sight of Nick. If he'd give Dahlia even a quarter of that concern, she might feel like all this was worth the trouble.

She shrugged. "Matt's doing really well. I

mean it," she said. "He's exercising like a fiend. It's amazing. It seems like he gets stronger and healthier every day. And Julie's there for him all the way. She's totally supportive." She couldn't help but emphasize the Julie part. Just in case Nick was getting any ideas in his head.

Nick smiled, the worry on his face giving way to relief, his green eyes softening. "It must be so hard for those guys."

"Yeah, it is. For all of us. I sort of feel like part of the extended family, actually." Since Matt's illness, Dahlia had been with them more than ever. Shuttling Julie to the hospital, hanging out with her when she needed a friend. Maybe having secretly paid Julie's tuition made her a little more attached, too, but the truth was, Dahlia really loved those guys. She saw how alone they were feeling, just the two of them, confused, scared, not sure what lay around the corner, and she wanted to help.

"I feel so useless. I wish there was something I could do."

Dahlia nodded sympathetically.

"Got any ideas?" Nick asked. "Every time I try to send a message, I get a pretty definite one back: 'Bug off!'"

Dahlia took a deep breath. Maybe she shouldn't get in the middle of this, but wasn't it time to put the past where it belonged? "Why don't you tell him yourself, Nick? In person.

Maybe he'd react differently than you think if he actually heard it from you, face-to-face."

"I tried that already. He totally snubbed me outside the movie theater."

"So try again," Dahlia suggested. "Like I said, his spirits are riding high these days. Why don't you talk to him at Club Night on Friday? He's always in a great mood then." All of a sudden, Dahlia realized she had inadvertently created the perfect situation for Nick to ask her out. The A on her paper was nothing compared to her lifetime A in flirting. She was a natural at that. "Matt says the band he lined up is really hot. It'll be a great night. I'll be there," she added, not as casually as she'd intended.

Nick seemed to freeze a moment, then shook his head. "I haven't been going to Club Night lately. I was afraid I was just making Matt feel lousy." He scratched the back of his head and let out a hefty sigh. "I don't know, maybe it would be best if I just stayed out of the whole thing. I mean, you said Matt was doing great and everything. I wouldn't want to stir up any bad feelings, you know?"

"Sure," Dahlia said flatly. "Look, I'll see you around, Nick. I've got to get going." She turned and headed for her mailbox, refusing to show Nick an ounce of her disappointment.

Why was he so impossible, anyway? Until Nick, everything with boys had been so cut and dried. He loved you or he didn't. And if he did, there was a guaranteed progression. First you looked at each other across the room a lot. Then you smiled at each other, then you went out, you kissed, and if you found out you liked each other—really liked each other—you went to bed. Eventually you broke up because he wasn't the right guy after all. And the whole thing started up again with the next guy.

The battle of voices in her head began banging away again. Dahlia could hear Paul Chase telling her that Nick wasn't worth all the trouble. Julie, meanwhile, insisted that Nick wouldn't be talking to her and teasing her if he didn't like her. And in the middle, Dahlia heard her heart, telling her that Nick was the one for her. One more chance. He probably didn't deserve it, but Dahlia was willing to give him one more chance to fall head over heels for her.

The Barn and Grill was packed as usual for a Friday night. The Grand Slam, Ohio's claim to extra-alternative rock, had been pumping their sound out for hours, and were still going strong. The band seemed to define loud—two wild, angry drummers, a seething electric guitarist, and a female lead singer, who also played bass, carried their music to the limit.

The crowd, a mix of students and locals, was hopping, their energetic pulse reverberating off the walls. A few months ago, these same customers had come to blows when tensions between the college students and the locals had reached their limit. But Club Night had a way of making everyone forget their problems, if only for as long as the band played.

Business at the Barn and Grill had never been better. Tonight's crowd could barely fit inside, and nobody had seemed to mind the dollar rise in the cover charge. As co-partner on Club Night with Jake and Pat, that alone would mean a noticeable amount of extra money in Matt's pocket at night's end. So why wasn't he happier?

Maybe it was because no one seemed to allow him to forget, even for a minute, the big "C" word. It was as if it was written on top of his big bald head: *I HAVE CANCER!* Matt had seen the signs even before he'd first gone in for his biopsy. People were acting uncomfortable around him. But it had gotten so much worse.

On one hand were the "wow, do I feel sorry for you" types. Pat was the leader of that group. Purposely not loading up his tray, sneaking orders over to tables on her own, it was as if she thought Matt should have stayed home in bed. She and Jake had hired Brian, a kid from school, to take over for Matt during his two-week hospital stays. But Pat had Brian helping out tonight, too. He wasn't splitting

Matt's tips or anything, just clearing tables and sweeping up.

"We need the extra help, because it's so busy," Pat had rationalized. Matt couldn't really say he loved bussing tables, but it hurt being treated so obviously like an invalid.

Then there were the long faces—Marcy and some of her friends, and most of Julie's friends from school. All Matt was doing was delivering burgers to someone, and there was Gwen, or Sarah, or one of the others on the dance floor, looking as though somebody had just died.

On the other hand, there was the half that just plain couldn't deal. With Jake, it was like the words *cancer* or *chemotherapy* didn't exist. If you didn't say them, or think them, they couldn't harm you. Bob and Scott, friends of Julie's from her old dorm, would order directly from Pat, then sneak into a corner to eat their burgers. They weren't the only ones who worked up a ten- or twenty-dollar tab without ever having Matt serve them. The clincher would be when they paid the bill and actually tipped him. For doing what? "Hey, here's a couple of bucks for having cancer."

Matt didn't know which kind of treatment was worse. Didn't people see him getting stronger all the time? He wanted to get up onstage himself and make a formal announcement. "Haven't you heard? My lump's all gone, and I'm not coughing anymore!" He laughed bitingly to himself as he wondered whether anybody else in the whole place could have done the workout he did earlier today, especially after an hour of radiation treatment, then come in and set up a rock concert, and then wait on tables. Doubtful. After running seven miles and doing a hundred-plus sit-ups and push-ups, most of these guys would probably crash out on the nearest couch for the rest of the day.

Matt sighed. He looked around for a needy customer, but they all seemed to be doing just fine on their own. Pat had sneaked another platter of food over to a table of kids near the door. And the band played on.

Through the throng of people on the dance floor, Matt spotted Julie. She was sitting at a table with Dahlia, Marion, and Fred. He didn't see a smile on a single one of their faces. Julie looked as if she wasn't hearing a note the band played.

That was the thing that upset Matt the most. He knew how scared Julie was. Sure, she tried to hide her fear, forcing smiles and promises of hope whenever she was around him, but it didn't hide the worry in her eyes.

He longed for them to shine brightly again, but he could only wait. A few months from now he'd come home from the hospital with a clean bill of health. Then he'd have the real Julie back again. The one with the knockout smile, soft, full cheeks, the big brown eyes that didn't hide her emotions. Soon.

Soon, but when? Matt tried not to let the frustration take hold of him, but it hurt, wondering how long he'd have to wait until he and Julie were happy together again, until they'd be able to make love together. Surely one day soon, this would all be behind them. Surely things would be the way they'd been before, wouldn't they?

Twelve

Julie and Matt stepped outside into the crisp, sunny day. Julie blinked. The light was clear and bright, the sky an intense blue. The air was still cold, but there was a hint of sweetness, a hint that spring was on the way. "Wow, nice day!"

"Yeah. Beautiful day to study dog poop." Matt laughed. He slung his arm around Julie's shoulder.

Julie put her arm under his leather jacket and around his waist. She drew extra close to him. He was still thinner than usual, but his muscles were well-delineated and hard as rock. He'd run another ten miles today and worked out in the gym, too. But this afternoon, he'd traded in his sneakers for his beat-up motorcycle boots. He was Julie's for the rest of the day.

"So? Where do we start, Boss?" he asked. He began searching the sidewalk, pulling Julie along Main Street. "Anything suspicious here? Anything offensive? Here! Right next to this tree. Excuse me, miss." He turned to face Julie, holding on to an invisible microphone. "Could you tell me what you think of *that*?" He pointed to the dog poop, then pushed the pretend microphone at Julie.

Julie giggled.

Matt scowled. "This is a serious issue, miss. Do you know that dog poop constitutes one quarter of the litter on our streets? That it contributes to the extreme acidic content of our soil? That it gets on your shoes and is really hard to get off—especially when you've got on sneakers with grooves in the soles?"

"Gross, Matt!"

"Well, that's really what the pooper-scooper law boils down to, doesn't it? I mean, who'd be opposed to it?"

"You'd be surprised. Some dog owners just don't want to have to deal with it. Plus, if they put the law into effect, then they have to get some police officer to make sure it's being obeyed. Of course, the tickets would help pay for the officer's time, but in some places, it's wound up costing the taxpayers money."

"Not to mention that some poor cop who draws doo-duty is going to be pretty bummed."

Julie laughed. "Copeland came up with a real doo-zy of an assignment this time, didn't he?"

Matt gave a loud groan. "I don't know if the jokes can get any worse. Don't we have some interviewing to do?"

"You mean, to doo-oo?" Julie said, breaking into hysterics. Matt let out a loud laugh, too. Maybe they weren't going to get a whole lot of work done, but it felt good to be laughing together over something so dumb. "All right, all right!" She held her hands up in the air. "Let's start with some of the people on the street. Then we can go door-to-door and get some opinions." She took a legal pad and pen out of her shoulder bag. "You know, this really isn't going to be so easy. How am I supposed to keep a straight face, anyway?"

"You're the reporter, Jules. Hey, how about them?" Matt pointed to a middle-aged couple coming around the corner in matching designer sweatsuits—powder-pink for her, navy for him. Pulling them along, straining at her leash, was a small, white-haired poodle, with a bow-shaped barrette—pink, to match the woman's outfit. Or was her outfit supposed to match the dog's barrette? Julie wondered.

"Perfect," she said, hurrying toward them. "Excuse me, ma'am . . . sir." They looked at her.

The poodle tugged at the leash and let out a sharp bark.

"My name is Julie Miller-Collins. This is my husband, Matt. I'm writing an article about the proposed pooper-scooper law, and I'd like to get the opinion of some of Madison's dog owners."

"Pooper-scooper?" the woman said.

"Yes. A law that will require owners to clean up after their dogs."

The woman wrinkled her nose. Somehow, Julie couldn't imagine her, tissue in hand, cleaning up after her dog. "Would you be for something like that, or against it?" Julie prodded.

"Oh, well . . ." the woman said.

"Oh, for heaven's sake," her husband put in. "Don't they have anything better to do around here than to pass laws against dog owners?"

Julie raised an eyebrow at Matt. He gave an almost imperceptible nod: *Yeah, you told me so.* She scribbled down what the man had said. "Then you're against the law?"

The man shrugged. The dog let out another bark.

"Lady Di!" the woman said. She looked at Julie and Matt. "Excuse us, but I think she wants to go." The three of them took off.

"Well, thank you for talking to us," Julie called after them. "When you got to go, you got to go," she added under her breath to Matt. "That *is* what this is about, isn't it?"

Matt laughed. "Lady Di?" he said incredulously.

They didn't have to move a step to get their next response. An older woman with curlers in her hair, carrying a bag of groceries, came right up to them. Excitedly, she pointed toward Lady Di and her owners. "You expect *us* to clean up after *them*? Treat the streets like it's their personal bathroom is what they do!" she said, stamping her foot on the ground. "It's downright disgusting! And you can print that Mrs. Edna Atwood said that. People should behave in a civilized way. And dogs should, too."

Julie and Matt stood transfixed before Mrs. Atwood. Julie wished she had a camera with her. One photo of the woman was all she'd need for inspiration when it came time to write her article.

Within an hour or so, Julie had almost filled up her pad. "Wow, I never thought this issue could yield so much ink," she said to Matt.

"Did you say 'stink'?" She and Matt both cracked up. "Yeah, I mean, now I have all the more reason to live. I have to see how this whole issue turns out," Matt added.

Julie's laughter stopped in her throat. "That's not funny."

Matt stopped laughing, too. He moved closer to her and took her hand. "Hey, Jules, I didn't mean anything by it. Really. Hang on.

I'm *going* to make it. I know I am."

"I know," Julie said, but she felt a sting of doubt.

"Listen, you've got to look at it this way," Matt said. "Some good stuff is coming out of this. I mean, our folks actually talked to one another for the first time in years."

Julie nodded. "That's true."

"And this whole thing is making me realize how incredible life is," Matt went on. "I mean, I always—I don't know—had fun, but it's like everything means more now. The sun, the sky, the cold—even the poop!"

Julie had to smile.

"No, really," Matt insisted. "I've been thinking about my life lately. You know—my future. I never really worried so much about it before. Never had to. Everything just sort of fell into place, you know? But now, it's kind of like I'm being given a second chance. I have to admit something to you."

Julie felt a tug of curiosity. "Yeah?"

"I've been thinking that maybe I'll take a class in the fall. Something that might help me run a business one day. Maybe I'll try an art class, too. You know, something I've never tried before."

"Really?" Julie's smile widened.

"Uh-huh. You think it's a good idea?"

"Definitely." Maybe Matt was right. Maybe

something good *could* come out of his illness—once he got better.

"I'm going to be fine," Matt said insistently. "Just fine."

Julie felt a shadow of doubt steal across her bright mood. It must have shown on her face.

"You don't believe me," Matt said.

Julie sucked in her breath. "I believe you. It's just that, Matt, sometimes I get scared." Okay, she'd said it. She'd finally said it. That was how she felt.

Matt was silent for a moment. "All right, Julie. I'll admit it. Sometimes I am, too. Real scared. But right now, it's a beautiful day and you're beautiful, and I'm alive. That's what counts most. You know what I'm saying?"

Julie nodded, even though her chest still felt tight with worry. Matt was right. They had to take things one day at a time.

Julie tried to remember how funny it had sounded last time: the bursar's office. Bursar. But as she sat in the hard chair in the outside office, the bursar's secretary typing as rapidly as machine-gun fire, she couldn't seem to find the humor in the word.

She repeated it in her mind. Bursar. The person in charge of finances. Bur-sar. If you said it enough, it became meaningless. But funny? Back in the fall, she and Matt had been in here trying not to crack up. Back in the fall, newly married, they'd been so starry-eyed that even being flat broke and not knowing how they were going to pay for Julie's tuition wasn't enough to make them stop laughing. Even the other day, researching her journalism article, lots of things had seemed funny. And Matt had said everything was going to be fine.

But it wasn't fine. Matt was one day closer to going back into the hospital, and her silly mood of the other day had disappeared. Two weeks in the hospital, two weeks out. Month after month. Julie frowned. She was still waiting for a paycheck—all of one hundred ninety dollars. Pretty dismal for a month's work at the dining hall. And Matt was only making half pay at the Barn and Grill. Even when the tips were good, even with Club Night profits, it didn't add up to enough. Not nearly enough. Julie cast a glance at the closed door to the inner office of the bursar. Thank heavens for short-term student loans. Scott, from Julie's old hall, liked to boast that the state of his CD collection owed a lot to these loans. Books, school supplies, what-have-you: You could borrow the money now, and they tacked it on to next semester's bill.

Which could certainly be a problem next semester. But right now, that seemed a long way off. A whole spring and summer away. By then, Matt might be all better. Or . . . no! Julie wasn't going to concentrate on anything but today. Things *did* have a way of working out. At least they had so far, for her and Matt.

The last time she'd come to this office with him, to ask for a tuition deferment, a way to pay for college bit by bit, they'd miraculously discovered that the tuition for her spring semester had been paid—anonymously. It was all so strange—her father's angry pronouncement about how Julie was on her own now that she had decided to get married, her mother's funny little hint over the phone last fall about her "little gift," as if it were no more than the Thanksgiving recipes she'd clipped and sent to Julie. And then, no talk of it again. Her mother had clammed up so fast when her dad had gotten on the phone that Julie had been afraid to try to mention it again. It was as if it had never happened.

Julie shifted around in her seat, absently watching the secretary's fingers flying over the keyboard of her computer. Why did her parents have to be so disapproving, so distant? Why did it take Matt's getting sick to melt some of their ice?

The phone near the computer rang—two short rings. The secretary picked it up, then looked over at Julie. "Ms. Miller-Collins, you can go in now."

Julie stood up as a short, wiry boy came out

of the bursar's office. She passed him and went inside.

"Hello, Ms. Miller-Collins," said the slender, gray-haired woman behind the bulky, wooden desk. "Nice to see you again."

"Hi, Mrs.—" Julie glanced at the plastic nameplate on the desk to refresh her memory. "—Jackson."

"How's married life?" Mrs. Jackson asked.

Julie was touched that the bursar remembered. But the question made her whole body go tense. Married life. In sickness and in health. *In sickness.* The corners of Julie's mouth turned down.

"Oh," Mrs. Jackson said softly. "I see. I'm sorry."

Julie shook her head. "No, it's not that. It's—Matt, my husband. He's sick." Mrs. Jackson looked concerned. "That's why I'm here," Julie explained. "All the medical bills—and the other bills . . . I was hoping—I mean, I know the short-term loan is really supposed to be for school stuff. . . ."

Mrs. Jackson gave a little frown. "Ms. Miller-Collins, why don't you sit down?" She indicated the armchair across from her desk. Julie nodded and perched herself on the edge of the chair. "Ms. Miller—Julie—what is the nature of your husband's illness?"

Julie bit her lip. There was something about

saying the word out loud, something so harsh and final. "He has—cancer."

Mrs. Jackson's features seemed to shift. "Oh, my! I'm so sorry."

Julie nodded.

Mrs. Jackson didn't say anything for a moment. She shook her head, picking up a stack of paper from her desk and straightening it. She let out an audible breath. "If I remember correctly, your husband is not a student here," she finally said.

"No," Julie answered, despondent.

"Well, strictly speaking, we're not supposed to give loans for noncollege purposes. But I think this is a special case."

Julie felt a breath of relief—as much relief as she could feel, considering the circumstances.

"You understand, of course, that we won't be able to issue you any new loans until this one is paid back."

"I understand," Julie echoed. She'd cross that bridge when she came to it. There was no other choice. Mrs. Jackson pushed an application form across the table, and Julie filled it out. "Thank you," Julie said, standing up as she handed back the completed form.

"You're welcome. One more thing, Julie. Have you discussed your financial situation with your family?" she asked. "It might be a good idea."

Julie nodded, but she knew neither she nor Matt would do it. Matt was afraid his father would force him to come back to Philadelphia, and while Julie did feel slightly closer to her family after her mother's phone call, they were still a long way from being one happy family.

"It should take a few days for your loan to go through," Mrs. Jackson said. "You'll get a letter when the check is ready."

Julie moved toward the door. "Thanks again."

Mrs. Jackson stood, too. "And, Julie? Good luck," she said.

Good luck. After all the treatments and loans and phone calls and worries, maybe that was all that it came down to. Luck. Good or bad.

Thirteen

Julie dipped the ice-cream scoop into the big plastic bucket of thick, gluey mashed potatoes and shook it out into a small white bowl. She prepared a half-dozen servings and put them up on the metal shelves of the service line. Library paste, Play-Doh, wet plaster—after a while, the stuff looked like anything but food. Julie smiled wryly, thinking of the underground industrial kitchen she and Matt had imagined connecting all schools and hospitals and company cafeterias.

"What's the big joke? Did you sneak something awful into the mashed potatoes?"

Julie looked up. Dahlia was leaning around the metal shelves. "Hey!" Julie greeted her. "Wow. What's the occasion?" Dahlia had on a midnight-blue knit turtleneck sweater and a matching ankle-length knit skirt that hugged every curve. Her coat was draped over her arm to reveal her outfit. Who said long skirts couldn't be sexy? Then again, anything looked sexy on Dahlia.

Dahlia shrugged. "Just dressing up for a little lunch. You never know who's going to show up." She arched her eyebrow.

"I haven't seen him in here today," Julie said.

"Oh." Dahlia pouted. "Well, maybe I'll go do a little studying in the library later."

"Second-floor study carrels," Julie advised. That used to be her favorite spot, too, but after that evening with Nick, she'd moved to another part of the library.

"Yeah, I know. And the far corner of the snack bar, second window from the right on the second floor of Old Wilder, Box 264 in the mail room . . ."

Julie laughed. "Dahlia, maybe you should just ask the guy on a date. It'd be a lot easier than going on a hunting expedition every day."

Dahlia shook her head. "And have him turn me down?"

"That ride home you gave him over fall break was four months ago!" Julie said. "I'm sure he's figured out he was wrong about you."

"Then he can ask *me* out. Meanwhile, I'll just hang around and drool from a reasonable distance. Besides, I think he's almost there. Then again, I could be totally wrong." Dahlia took a dish of corn. "How's Matt doing?"

Julie sighed. It was so much easier to talk about other people's problems. "Fine, I guess. I mean, he's got a deadly disease, but besides that . . ." she cracked weakly.

"He still jocking out?" Dahlia asked. "I was looking out my window and I saw him running past Wilson Hall the other day."

"Yeah. He's up to about a million miles a day. Two million on his bike. Ten thousand push-ups and four million sit-ups. His body looks great, and he'll bite off anyone's head who treats him like he's sick."

"I guess that's good," Dahlia said. "Thinking strong."

Julie shrugged. "I don't know. I mean, it's definitely good that he has a positive attitude. Definitely. But sometimes it's like he's pretending he's not sick at all, you know? Maybe he needs to break down and cry once in a while." Julie dished out portions of spinach as she and Dahlia talked. "Or maybe I'm just saying that because that's what I seem to be doing about every ten minutes these days. I don't know, I think I just want to take care of him—feel like I'm doing something, and he's Mr. Independent. Doesn't need me, doesn't need anyone. Down on the floor, doing another round of push-ups. Making a zillion phone calls to book a hot band for Club Night. He never stops for a second." Julie took a deep breath. She realized her voice was gathering volume and some of the kids pushing their trays through the lunch line were shooting her looks. "Wow, I didn't mean to sound off like that," she said.

"Hey, I'm the jerk who's standing here moaning about you-know-who, when you guys . . ."

Julie waved off Dahlia's words. "No. Come on, you know I need to talk about other stuff. If I think about this all the time, I'll just lose it."

"Yeah, well—" Dahlia said. The conversation seemed to stall out. Julie was getting used to it. She needed to forget about Matt's illness for a few minutes, but next to that terrifying, heavy-duty topic, everything else seemed so unimportant.

"So, you have any plans for next weekend?" Julie asked.

Dahlia shook her head. "I guess I need to hit the books. I mean, I actually sort of want to. Now that I'm figuring out what's going on in my class on the Sistine Chapel, it's pretty cool. Boy, if anyone had told me I'd be spending my weekends studying . . ."

"Well, if you feel like it, you can come over and study at my house. I've got to get to work writing about dog poop."

"Serious stuff they teach us in college," Dahlia commented.

Julie gave a little laugh. "Really. Anyway, Matt'll be back in the hospital by then. I could use the company."

Dahlia nodded. "It's a date. And the best one I'm likely to get."

Julie shook her head. "Give yourself some credit. One day the guy's going to open his eyes."

"That positive attitude, right?" Dahlia said with a hopeless sigh.

Julie nodded.

"Yeah, well . . . You, too, okay?"

"Okay," Julie echoed. "See you, Dahlia. And thanks."

Julie watched Dahlia carry her tray out to the dining hall. *Have a positive attitude.* But how? Julie frowned. Maybe she should start doing millions of push-ups, too.

"If he calls, tell him I'm sleeping." Marion looked guiltily at her roommate, Susan. It wasn't like Marion to lie, but she didn't really know how else to handle it. If she didn't get some studying done soon, she'd never catch up. She knew Fred was going to worry when she didn't show up at the library tonight. But he'd be crushed if she told him she needed a night off.

"I don't mean to pry—" Susan took a seat on

the edge of Marion's bed. "How could you pass up all those wonderful kisses?" she asked, blushing.

Marion put her pen down on her desk and turned her chair around to face Susan. "It's just that boys seem to have a one-track mind. At least Fred does. Don't get me wrong. Kissing is great! But—oh, I don't know—it's just that I haven't gotten any real studying done since our first kiss, and neither has Fred."

Susan covered her mouth and let out a soft, shy giggle. "Lucky you. I wouldn't mind not studying or playing the violin for a night, either, if it meant that."

It wasn't that Susan couldn't find a guy. It wasn't that she didn't have crushes. She did. Marion knew that for a fact. Most recently, a cellist that she knew from the orchestra had caught her eye.

Pretty, with long, shiny black hair and smooth skin, Susan was fun and interesting to talk to, once she got over her initial shyness. The problem was her parents. Susan came from a traditional Korean family. So traditional that her mother and father had actually arranged a marriage for her, like in the old days. Even a casual date was out of the question, the way Susan told it. Her parents wouldn't allow it. One day, the son of a business associate of her father's back in Seoul, a boy who Susan had never even met, would become her husband. Susan said that her parents weren't going to get away with it, but at the same time, she loved them. She didn't want to hurt them by disobeying their wishes. If only she could figure out how to back out graciously.

Marion didn't envy Susan. Still, Susan did have plenty of time for homework and studying the violin. And this semester she'd taken up still-life painting, she was in the choir, and she even was learning to bowl on Friday nights.

Marion, meanwhile, spent most of her time locked at the lips with Fred. Delicious kisses, all of them, but they did start to get a little stale after a while.

"It's pretty funny in a way, isn't it?" Marion said. "You and me, I mean. You want a boyfriend, but can't have one, and I have one, but—" She stopped herself short of finishing the sentence. She *did* want a boyfriend. The one she had. Fred. She just wanted him a little less.

Just then the phone rang. She stared at it, not able to summon the courage to pick it up. Susan went to answer it, looking back at Marion, unsure of what to say. Marion furiously waved a hand, mouthing the words, "I'm sleeping."

"Hello," Susan whispered, extra softly. "I'm sorry I can't talk louder, Fred, but Marion's sound asleep. I guess she was studying, because there's a book right next to her on the bed. I'll tell her you called."

As she hung up the phone, they both looked at each other sheepishly. "Thanks," Marion said, breathing a guilty sigh of relief. But she knew she couldn't keep doing this. Sooner or later, she'd have to talk to Fred. But first, she'd have to figure out what she wanted.

Fourteen

They were both trying to pretend that it was just like any other night. Walking down Main Street, holding hands, on their way to see a movie. A boy and a girl on a typical date. But Julie was squeezing Matt's hand just a little too hard, and Matt was just a little too intense about lapping up enough of everything to last him through two weeks in the hospital.

"Wow! Great sky!" he said, tilting his head up as they strolled across the town green. "Isn't it?"

Julie looked up with him. In the absence of moonlight, the stars stood out like tiny, brilliant gems against pure black. The Milky Way was a path of soft silver from one edge of the night to the other. "Yeah, it's beautiful. Remember that time junior year when we rode out to that mountaintop in the Poconos to look at the sky?"

Matt gave a soft laugh. "Hey, what kind of guy would forget his first kiss with the woman he loves?" He put his arm around her shoulder. "We were standing just like this."

"You were pointing out Orion's belt," Julie said. "I was sort of looking up at the sky and sort of looking over at you at the same time." Julie saw Matt smile as she did the same thing now.

"And then I turned and looked at you, too. . . ." Matt said.

Julie met his gaze and put a gloved hand on his cheek. They drew closer. She felt a surge of love. Their lips met. She drank in his kiss, her eyes open to the stars around them. She tried to memorize the moment, make every detail strong enough in her mind to hold on to it until Matt got out of the hospital again. The smell of chimney smoke on the cool air, the warmth and moist softness of his lips, the distant sound of people laughing over on the campus side of the Green.

Their arms still circled around each other, they continued to walk—slowly, without speaking—simply feeling each other so close. Julie knew she wasn't going to be able to concentrate much on the movie they were going to see, but it didn't matter. She just wanted to have Matt near her. Besides, as usual, the Apollo was showing something she'd seen already.

A handful of people were milling around under the marquee. As she and Matt approached the ticket window, Julie tried to remember what happened in the movie.

"Two, please," Matt told the pudgy-faced man in the little booth. He reached into the pocket of his jeans for his wallet. As he paid for the tickets, Julie looked around. A mother and her two kids were going into the theater. A group of Madison students she recognized from the dining hall were standing around outside. A couple was crossing the street toward the theater. And behind them, his lanky stride immediately recognizable, was Nick. Julie felt herself tense up.

Nick was coming off the Green, walking quickly. Julie could tell he hadn't spotted her and Matt yet. She wanted to grab Matt's arm and hustle him inside the theater as quickly as possible. But Matt was calmly taking his change with the tickets, putting his wallet away, thanking the man in the ticket booth. Nick looked up as he crossed the street. In that moment, he saw them.

Julie felt trapped. She watched Nick focus on Matt, then look back at her. Their gazes locked. She raised her hand in a little wave. What else could she do? Pretend she hadn't seen him? But this was Matt's last night at home. They were trying so hard to have an enjoyable, relaxing evening.

Nick was coming toward them. What else could *he* do? Tickets in hand, Matt turned. He seemed to follow Julie's gaze. She sensed his whole body tighten up. He took a few steps away from the ticket booth, his eyes on Nick. Julie trailed after him, afraid to look at his face.

Nick took a few more steps before he raised his own hand in greeting. He closed the gap between them. "Hi." He smiled nervously.

Matt didn't say a word.

"Hi," Julie said with forced brightness.

Nick's green-eyed gaze went from Matt to Julie, back to Matt. "It's good to see you," Nick said genuinely.

Matt stood like a statue.

"How are you feeling?" Nick asked him.

"Fine." One hard, heavy syllable.

Julie cringed at Matt's coldness. It was as if all the anger and frustration that had been building inside him since he'd gotten sick was suddenly turned on Nick. She couldn't blame him, though. She could see how much Matt hurt. If only she could erase that one evening with Nick that never should have happened. Maybe she deserved to be caught in a crossfire. But why did it have to be tonight, of all nights?

Nick was still trying to reach out. "I've been thinking about you, man," he said.

Please let Matt accept his peace offering, Julie thought. *Not just for me.* Matt needed real friendship right now, the kind he'd once had with Nick.

But Matt rebuffed him again. "I don't need anyone's sympathy."

Nick looked as if Matt had slapped him. Matt didn't wait for Nick to rebound. He grabbed Julie's arm roughly. "I don't want to miss the beginning of the movie," he said, even though he'd already seen it twice.

"See you, Nick," Julie said miserably.

"See you," Nick said stiffly. "I'm pulling for you, Matt," he called after them.

"Spare me," Matt said under his breath, as they went through the Apollo's glass doors.

Julie shook off Matt's hand. "He was trying to be nice. He really does care, you know."

"Yeah. I'm sure he does. He cares about how I might be out of the picture one of these days."

Julie felt a wave of anger wash over her. "That's a really awful thing to say."

Matt shrugged.

"You know, people are trying to be there for you—to help you, and you just push everyone away!" Julie's voice came out louder than she'd meant it to.

Matt stared at her. "I don't need any help. Especially not his help. I'm fine, okay?"

Julie blinked back a tear. "No, it's not okay. I'm really sick of pretending that there's nothing wrong, when there is. You're going into the hospital tomorrow. Do you want me to act like you're going on vacation? Do you think this whole thing is so easy for me?"

Matt turned to go into the darkened theater. Julie followed him, the tears beginning to flow.

Matt lay in his hospital bed, nausea pulsating through him in crashing, unstoppable waves. Racked with pain, he tried to find a comfortable position while he worked his way through the aftereffects of the chemo. But nothing could ease the nightmares of the past few hours of treatment.

The orange liquid—CAD—a hybrid. But what was it, really? How could a few letters, a few chemicals, make him feel so awful?

Matt had learned all about the complicated terminology relating to his disease and the treatment of it, figuring that if he could demystify all the mumbo-jumbo, bring cancer down to a human level, it would make it easier to deal with. But lying there now, after having vomited ferociously for nearly three hours, he was rendered helpless. The two hundred rads of radiation he'd been pumped with, the one thousand milligrams of cytoxan, adriamycin, and DTIC—how could you demystify something like that? The protocol, the prescribed method of treatment, had taken control of him, of both his body and his mind.

The wretched, metallic taste in his mouth wouldn't go away. He could feel his insides beginning to go into convulsions again. He struggled to fight back another round of vomiting, but it was useless. Lacking the strength even to get himself to the bathroom, he reached for his bedpan and emptied his body of more poison.

Today was only day one of fourteen successive days of this living inferno. Matt didn't know how he could possibly continue. How could he subject himself to this kind of torture? Furthermore, how did he even know that the chemo was making him better? It was really the exercise, more than anything else, that was keeping him going.

Fourteen more days. He'd sworn to Julie, Pat, Leon, and everybody else that he was feeling great. Stronger than ever. But they all seemed to look at him doubtfully.

Matt caught a glimpse of his little friend Danny in the bed next to his, sleeping off this morning's treatment. Matt knew Danny looked up to him, so he had requested that they be roommates during their hospital stays. And they'd become fast friends. Matt was taken by

Danny's zest for life, even under the frightening circumstances they shared. After two years, Danny was a real pro at this. He'd even laugh about the CAD mixture afterward, referring to it as his morning shot of orange juice. "Some kids drink OJ for breakfast, I get it fed to me through a tube," he'd said.

Poor guy. Every waking moment was filled with dreams and visions of life as a regular kid. The Chicago Cubs pennant that hung over his bed was Danny's beacon of hope. The autographed baseball, signed by the whole Cubs team, was like his crystal ball. Danny would grasp it in his weak hands and pretend that his future was filled with happiness. And what was so wrong with that, anyway? Didn't every kid have the right to want a regular life?

But Matt knew that every kid didn't get one. It was so unfair. Matt cringed at the thought of Danny having to spend his days shuttled back and forth between home and a cancer ward.

And what about Matt? The terrifying thought that he'd been trying so hard to keep down began to surface: Was that what was in store for him, too? Dr. Zinn had said that if everything went well, he'd be cured in three to six months. And if it didn't go well?

The ugly word forced itself to the forefront of his mind. Death. If things didn't go right, he'd die. *No,* Matt told himself. *Not me.* He shouldn't even think it. But blocking out the fear of dying was getting harder and harder to do. Death—Matt dying—*was* a reality. After all, what did cancer patients do best? They died!

Matt realized that his cheeks were wet. It was the first time he'd cried since being diagnosed with cancer. For a moment the taste of the salty tears was comforting, but as the thought of death continued to intrude, a feeling of emptiness prevailed.

Death. The word pounded away inside his head. Wasn't that what all the people in Madison were seeing every time they looked at him with such sorrow in their eyes? Wasn't that what the extra fifty dollars in tips at the end of the week was all about? Isn't that why Julie would grasp his hand so tightly?

Last night, outside the movie theater, she'd practically given up on him. Julie had lost hope. How could he expect her to understand? How could anybody—any healthy person—know what it was like to be fighting cancer? They couldn't possibly understand what it felt like to be pumped full of poisonous chemicals fourteen days in a row. Or to be holed up in a cancer ward half the time, or to lose the ability and the desire to make love.

Matt felt another giant wave of nausea coming over him. "No!" he whispered, his voice urgent in the cold hospital room. *Not me,* he vowed. He wasn't going to end up like Danny, a step away from death. No! Matt wasn't going to lose this battle. Life was too great.

He fought his way out of bed and knelt down on the hard, cold tile floor. He let his weight fall on his arms and he stretched his legs out full. Push-ups. Exercise was the only way. Beating cancer was a one-man, full-time job. That's just the way it was. Matt had to focus every minute on staying healthy and strong.

He struggled through the first few push-ups. His stomach still rumbled with sickness. The story he'd read about the guy who'd become a champion canoe racer while going through chemo came into mind. That guy was living a regular, healthy life now—his story was proof positive. Matt took a deep breath and directed all his thoughts and energy on the idea of building strength. Without the will to survive, it couldn't be done.

Fifteen

Julie stared at the titles she'd crossed out of her notebook. *Here's the Poop. Doo the Right Thing.* Without Matt, it didn't seem very funny. Here she was, trying to write about dog poop, and Matt was sitting under some huge machine or moaning in pain on his hospital bed. She threw down her pen. "It's not fair," she muttered.

Across her kitchen table, Dahlia looked up from a large, thick book. "What?" she said distractedly. Usually when they got together to study, Dahlia wanted to do anything but. Gossip, pig out on chocolate-fudge cookies, listen to music. But tonight she actually seemed interested in that big, fat art book and the piles of Xeroxed magazine articles. Julie was the one who couldn't sit still.

"I can't concentrate on this," Julie said. "I

just can't do my schoolwork. I can't think." She pushed her notebook away from her.

"Why don't you call Matt and say hi?" Dahlia asked.

Julie pictured him, his face bloated and pale against the white bedding and green walls, little Danny lying weak in the bed next to his. She sighed. "I don't know. He was so . . . far away when I went to visit him yesterday. He spent practically the whole time talking to Danny about baseball. I never even knew Matt was such a fan."

"Julie, all guys are into baseball. It's like they're born knowing about it." Dahlia brushed a hand through her long, blond hair. "I guess it's understandable. I mean, if I were in Matt's situation, I don't think I'd want to think about being sick too much, either."

"Yeah, but where does that leave me?" Julie's voice rose. She hadn't realized what a spark of anger was smoldering inside her. "It's as if there's nothing I can do for him. Except pay the bills." She cast an exasperated look at the pile of white envelopes stacked on the table near her notebook. "And I'm not even doing that very well. The rent's already overdue. And the— Oh, never mind. It's the same sad story."

Dahlia eyed the pile, too. Then she flashed Julie a sympathetic look. "Maybe you just need to get out of here. You want to go and get a snack or something?"

Julie thought about how a month ago, when Matt was first diagnosed, it was almost unbearable to see people around her going on with their lives as usual. Now she was beginning to find that it was almost a relief, a chance to get away from her own worries, her own pain, and just feel like part of the regular world for a little while. "I could go for an ice-cream sundae at the Black Angus," she said. "If I can pull you away from that book. Or are you daydreaming about going to Rome with Nick again?"

Dahlia feigned a hurt expression. "Well, I wouldn't turn the guy down if he asked me, but as a matter of fact, this stuff about the Sistine Chapel is getting really interesting. There's this painter who lives in Rome who actually stopped sleeping at night because he was so freaked out that they were ruining Michelangelo's work instead of cleaning it. Can you believe it? Some guy getting insomnia about art that was made over five centuries ago! It's pretty intense."

Julie arched an eyebrow. "Fascinated by school, an A on the last test—Dahlia, are you feeling okay?"

Dahlia stuck her tongue out. "Well, if Nick's not going to take me to Italy, I've got to get *something* out of this class."

Julie chuckled.

"Good," Dahlia said, getting up and reaching for the coat she'd put over the back of her chair. "At least I made you laugh."

Julie got up, too. "Don't think I don't know how lucky I am to have such a good friend," she said seriously.

Dahlia waved her hand through the air as if to brush off the praise.

"No, really," Julie said. "Nick really ought to wake up and smell the coffee."

"Please—cappuccino, Julie," Dahlia corrected. "You know I only go for the best."

Julie giggled. "Dahlia, can't you take a compliment? I think I need to have a talk with that boy about you."

"Don't you dare!" Dahlia said. "I'll kill you if you say a word. Now, what about that sundae?"

"I don't know . . ."

"Come on, Julie. My treat."

Julie smiled. Dahlia really was the best. Julie didn't know what she would have done without her through all of this.

Julie pushed open the door that led from the bottom landing of her stairwell to Secondhand Rose. The string of bells over the door chimed noisily.

"Hello?" Emily Holmes's sweet voice preceded her appearance between racks of neatly hung vintage clothes. "Oh, Julie, dear." Julie stepped farther inside toward her landlady. The store smelled of freshly cleaned clothes with a faint trace of musky perfume.

"How are you?" Mrs. Holmes asked, concern on her deeply lined face and in her clear, blue eyes. She wore a pale-pink beaded sweater and a pair of old jeans, her white hair in a braid that she wrapped around her head like a crown.

"Hi, Mrs. Holmes," Julie said. "I'm okay. I guess." She glanced around the store. The racks seemed fuller than usual. "New shipment?"

"I went on a buying trip over the weekend," Mrs. Holmes said. "There's a lovely blue velveteen dress that I think would look perfect on you."

Julie shook her head. "I better not," she said. Secondhand Rose had some beautiful things. The shimmery, cream-colored dress Julie had gotten married in was from here, and so were the antique silver wedding bands that she and Matt wore. Julie wanted to look around, but she couldn't. "I mean, we're behind on the rent as it is. Which is what I wanted to talk to you about—I'm really sorry, Mrs. Holmes." Julie felt awful. Mrs. Holmes was the nicest landlady anyone could have. Julie hated to ask for an extension on the rent, but what other choice did she have?

Mrs. Holmes's brow wrinkled. "Behind? But

you put the envelope under the door just this morning."

"Excuse me?" What was Mrs. Holmes talking about? She might have powder-white hair, and she wore bifocals sometimes, but she was far from out of it.

Mrs. Holmes studied her face. "Oh, you didn't? Well, perhaps Matt left it. He must have made quite a lot of tips this week to pay the rent in cash. By the way, how is he doing, Julie?"

"Cash?" Julie felt a wave of confusion. "But, Mrs. Holmes, Matt went back into the hospital this weekend. He couldn't have left the money for you."

Mrs. Holmes's face clouded over. "Oh, he did? Julie, I'm sorry. I didn't realize it was time again. But then how—" Mrs. Holmes looked confused now, too.

"Are you sure?" Julie asked. "Maybe it wasn't our rent."

"But, dear, the rent voucher I typed up for you was in that envelope."

"The voucher?" That was impossible. It was upstairs in her apartment, on the table with the rest of the bills. She'd seen it, right on top of the pile last night when Dahlia had been over and—

Dahlia! She was the only one who knew the rent was past due. Suddenly Julie wasn't sure she'd even noticed the pile of bills when she'd wolfed down a bowl of cereal at the kitchen table before morning classes.

"Excuse me, Mrs. Holmes," she said, whirling around and heading for the door.

"Perhaps you have a secret angel looking out for you," Mrs. Holmes called after her.

Julie raced out of the shop and bolted upstairs to her apartment. *If I do, I have a pretty good idea who that angel is,* she thought. She fumbled with her keys and rushed inside. The kitchen table was still littered with schoolbooks, her empty cereal bowl and spoon, and a crumpled-up napkin. But the pile of envelopes was gone! Every last one of them.

Julie felt a rush of gratitude and surprise and discomfort all rolled up in one powerful wash of emotion. Dahlia was too much! Julie remembered the way she'd eyed the stack of bills when she was over the night before. She must have grabbed them and stuffed them in her book bag as they were going out to the Black Angus. Talk about good friends! But Julie couldn't take Dahlia's money. Even if she had plenty of it to spend. It just wasn't right.

Wasn't it more than enough that Dahlia taxied Julie to the hospital almost every day? That she'd drop everything and come right over when Julie felt especially lonely and frightened? That she made Julie laugh?

And even before Matt had gotten sick, Dahlia had helped out in dozens of little, and not so little, ways. From gifts of furniture and kitchenware to a Sunday brunch out for all of them. Too many people judged Dahlia by her flash and style and her father's bank account, and came up with the wrong idea. The real Dahlia was a loyal friend—and generous to a fault.

But even Dahlia must have known she'd gone overboard this time. Why else would she have been so secretive about what she'd done?

Julie grabbed her coat and headed out toward the quad and Wilson Hall to look for her.

Sixteen

Matt gritted his teeth and pulled his shoulders up from the floor again. Hands clasping the back of his head, he touched his right elbow to his left knee, then his left elbow to his right knee, then eased himself back down to the ground. As he repeated the cycle of sit-ups over and over again, he began to taste the perspiration dripping down his face. Good, wholesome, salty sweat. He inhaled and exhaled deeply. Exhaustion, but it was a healthy feeling of exhaustion.

There was a knock on his door. "Anybody home?" came a friendly voice. Dr. Zinn, clipboard in hand, stood in the doorway. His youthful appearance always came as a bit of a shock to Matt. In a lab coat, with a stethoscope around his neck, he almost looked as if he was playacting. All the same, Matt knew he meant business.

"Oh, there you are," the doctor said, peering over Matt's bed frame. A slightly surprised look came over him when he spotted Matt on the floor.

"Hey, how's it going?" Matt asked, in between a couple of sit-ups.

"That's what I was going to ask you. I thought you were the patient, after all."

Matt laughed. He sat up and let out a big breath. "Phew. Yeah. Well, I feel pretty good. Real good, I mean. This morning was another nightmare, though."

"Chemo can get pretty rough," the doctor said.

"I hope you're going to tell me the minute I'm all better, because if I have to do one extra day of it, I'll kill somebody."

"That bad, huh? Well, I'm not surprised. Your body's being run through the mill. I'm proud of you though, Matt. You're a real trouper. Most people either threaten to quit by this time or else they actually do quit. A lot of them think it's too cruel to go through."

"I can relate to that. If you'd seen me this morning I'd definitely have been in one of those groups. But I did some big-time thinking, you know? I'm going all the way with this. I'm going to survive it, and fast," Matt promised.

"Great. That's what I like to hear."

But Matt noticed the doctor eyeing the clipboard he had with him. He didn't like the serious look on the doctor's face. "Problem?" he asked.

Dr. Zinn smiled. "I thought you were a rock-and-roll promoter. You never told me you were a part-time psychologist."

"I just saw you looking at my chart, that's all. Isn't that what that is?"

Dr. Zinn nodded. "I was looking at your recent blood count. This was just done this morning. Remember when I told you what would happen after a while?"

"Sure," Matt said. "You said there was a chance that my red and white count would decrease."

"And?"

"And that I'd feel a little weaker and be more susceptible to getting sick—infections, stuff like that."

"Smart boy. That's right. Your immune system would become more vulnerable to disease. Well, it's nothing to really worry about, Matt, but your count, as of this morning, is on the low side."

"Okay. But it's like you said, that's what's supposed to happen, right?" Matt asked.

"Exactly, but—"

"But what?" Matt felt a sudden shiver creeping up his spine. Something had to be wrong.

"Matt, how many sit-ups have you done today?"

"Almost two hundred. And one hundred push-ups," he announced proudly.

The doctor's eyes opened wide with surprise.

"Too many?" Matt asked.

"That's not your idea of a mellow workout, is it? When I saw you a few days ago I seem to remember telling you it would be a good idea to ease up a little."

"You said if I didn't feel up to it, I shouldn't feel like I had to exercise. But I do feel up to it. I feel strong. I feel great," Matt insisted. "I don't feel sick or anything. As soon as the chemo wears off, I feel as strong as ever."

"I think you missed my point." Dr. Zinn frowned. "Extreme exhaustion and chemo treatment just don't mix well. The more you exercise, by definition, the more you're working your body toward exhaustion."

"But I feel great. Really, I do," Matt protested.

"Matt, sometimes your mind can play tricks on you."

"So you're saying I'm not in good shape."

"No, it's not that. What I'm saying is that you are filled with determination. So much so that your head might be fooling your body into ignoring the symptoms. You tell me that you're not feeling exhausted. And actually, I believe you. You *do* feel strong. But your chart is showing me otherwise. The blood count's too low for your system not to be depleted. The results from this morning are just a little warning signal. It's time to be careful."

"So what, then?" Matt asked, feeling the walls beginning to close in on him. "You want me to lie around in bed till I die?"

"Now wait a minute," the doctor said, the frustration showing on his face. "Who said anything about dying?"

"You said my chart was bad."

"What I said was that your blood count's down. Slightly. That's normal," Dr. Zinn said, emphasis on normal.

"Normal. Yeah, right. You call this normal? Lying around puking my brains out all morning long." Matt couldn't hold back his own frustration.

"Hey, what happened to the positive thinker?"

"I guess he just got reminded that he's got cancer, that's what."

"That's right, Matt, you *do* have cancer." Dr. Zinn paused a moment. A heavy silence filled the air. "Come on, Matt, don't give up now. I came in here this afternoon to tell you how well you were doing. I really don't get the attitude."

"Okay, fine." Matt picked himself up off the

floor and got back into bed. He wasn't about to admit it now, but maybe he did feel a little overtired from his workout. Usually after a hundred sit-ups and push-ups he'd barely feel it. But his muscles did feel somewhat strained, and he felt a little woozy. Or was that his head talking after hearing the news about his blood count? "How about passing me the phone, then, Doc? I might as well make some business calls."

Dr. Zinn stood there with his arms crossed, shaking his head—a decisive no.

"Now what? I can't even call a couple of band agents? Should I call the nurse in so she can dial for me?" Matt asked, his voice filling with sarcasm.

"Okay, I'm going to try once more," the doctor said, suddenly sounding as tired as Matt felt. "Right at the very beginning of this whole thing, we made a deal. We said that it would be okay for you to start worrying when you saw me worrying."

"And you're worrying, is that it?"

"I'm worrying because I'm seeing you try too hard. You want to get better and stronger all at once. It's only natural to feel that way. But it's just not possible. Chemo doesn't work like that. It has to run its course."

"The only time I really feel bad, though, is during the treatment. It feels like poison," Matt said.

"It is poison." Dr. Zinn let out a heavy sigh. "I have an idea of how hard this must be for you. You feel the chemo every day and it feels like it's killing you. Trust me, the chemo is killing your cancer, and that's all. Let it work, Matt. Let it do its thing. You understand what I'm saying?"

Matt shook his head. "If I'm still sick, I wish I felt it. This thing is so crazy. My tests say I have cancer. You say it. But I feel—"

"But you *are* still sick," Dr. Zinn insisted. "Unfortunately, that's the bottom line. Don't deny it, Matt. You can't run around pretending that you're not sick, or you're begging for trouble."

Matt threw his hands in the air in frustration. "So no work phone calls, no push-ups or sit-ups. What, then?"

"R and R. Read a book. What about all those great mysteries that Julie brought you? Or watch the tube—a game, a movie."

"Great, turn me into a couch potato," Matt huffed.

"Matt, it's only temporary. Take it easier until your blood count goes up. Why don't you take a hint from your friend over there?" He pointed to Danny, who'd been sleeping soundly through the entire conversation. "If you rest now, your body will get stronger for tomorrow's session."

Matt was silent. His whole goal was to maintain his regular life while he underwent the treatment, and now that was being taken from him.

"I'll be back to see you in a few days," the doctor said. "You still with me?"

Matt gave a little nod, but his silent brooding continued.

"Now be good, huh? We can beat this thing, Matt. But only if we work together at it. Get some rest and be good to yourself. If you can't stand lying in bed, walk around a little, okay? Do a few push-ups," he said. "But just a few. No more marathons. I don't want to have to put a twenty-four-hour security watch on you." The doctor gave a friendly nod and left the room.

Matt made a muscle with his right arm. He was the strongest cancer patient around, and he wanted to keep it that way. The news couldn't have been worse. Staying fit was what was getting him through all the misery of the treatment. That was obvious to Matt. Didn't anybody else understand how important it was? Dr. Zinn had just cut off his lifeline, as if it were no big deal. Why not just take away his food and water, too? Everyone around him seemed to treat him like an invalid—and now his own doctor was doing it, as well.

Matt felt the anger coursing through him. Twelve more days and who knows how many months of horror lay ahead, and his only solace had been stolen from him. How would he maintain his sanity now? By lying flat on his back, watching talk shows and reruns on the tube? Sleeping twenty hours a day? He'd heard so much about how chemotherapy attacked your mind as well as your body. He hadn't let it happen to him, but now he had no choice.

"I can't let you do it," Julie said. She took off her jacket and plunked it down on her old bed in her old dorm room, on Dahlia's antique quilted comforter. When Julie had moved out, Dahlia had moved from the outside to the inside room of the divided double, along with her collection of posters of New York City. The Brooklyn Bridge, the skyline at night, an ad to "Keep the Big Apple Shiny" that Dahlia had taken from a subway car.

"I actually had to ride the subway to get that one," Dahlia had said.

Now Dahlia began pacing the room, looking at her posters, out the window, anywhere but at Julie. "Can't let me do what?" she asked, her false innocence as transparent as glass.

"Oh, come on, Dahlia. You know. It's a really generous thing to do. Incredibly generous. And totally nice. But that's *our* rent, *our* phone bill, Matt's medical expenses."

Dahlia was silent.

"Look, they were on the table last night, and then they were gone. You were the only person who's been over."

Dahlia shrugged.

"Come on, fess up, Dahlia. You know that I know."

Dahlia let out a huffy breath. "Well, what if it *was* me?"

"I appreciate what you're trying to do. Really. But it's not right."

"Why not?"

"So you admit it, then," Julie said.

"Look, Julie, do you know how much it costs to keep Clover up at a stable in Westchester? To feed and groom her? And Daddy gives me money for that as if it's nothing."

Julie wrinkled her forehead. "Clover? I don't see what that has to do with what we're talking about."

"Look, the point is that her upkeep costs a lot more than the monthly rent on your apartment, that's for sure," Dahlia said. "And Clover's just a horse."

"Is that right? Gee, Dahlia, I got the feeling she was the most important member of your family, from the way you talked."

Dahlia grinned. "Well, she is. But that's beside the point."

Julie laughed and shook her head. "Listen, you're an incredible friend. But I can't let you pay those bills. They're mine—and Matt's."

"Too late," Dahlia said matter-of-factly. "Not only can I, but I already have. I just wanted to help in whatever way I could."

"You've been helping me all along. Just being there for me. You'll have to let me pay you back," Julie said firmly.

Dahlia arched an eyebrow. "Except I happen to know that you don't have anything to pay me back with. Listen, Julie, why can't you just accept a little present? Say 'thank you' and that's that."

Julie let out a big breath, her shoulders rising and falling. "Dahlia, don't you think you've done enough? You go and furnish half our apartment. You shuttle me to the hospital and back and wait in the car so I can visit with Matt in private. You hang out with me—that's the most important."

"I can afford it," Dahlia said, frustration surfacing in her voice.

"It's the principle of the thing," Julie argued. "I just don't feel right about it."

"Principle? And how do you expect to pay your bills with principles? You know I don't expect you to come in here and kiss my feet or anything, but I do something nice and you make me feel like I committed a crime or something." Dahlia's voice was starting to rise.

Julie drew her mouth into a tight line. How

could she make Dahlia understand? "Look, we're friends. Best friends. I'm not . . . your charity case."

Dahlia grimaced. "You think I'm trying to . . . to buy our friendship." Her words were hard and angry.

"No, I didn't say anything of the kind!" Julie shot back.

"Did anyone ever tell you how stubborn you are? You know, I've paid your bills before, and if I have to I'll—" Dahlia slapped a hand across her mouth.

"Before?" Julie mouthed, the sound barely coming out of her mouth. "You've paid my bills before? Oh, my God!" It hit her like a punch in the stomach. *Her tuition!* The tuition that her mother had never really said she'd paid! Julie stared at Dahlia. Compared to paying the tab for second semester, taking care of that pile of bills really was a little present. "My tuition!" Julie gasped.

Dahlia looked down at the small Persian rug she'd had sent from home at the beginning of the year.

"Tell me the truth," Julie demanded. "You paid my second-semester tuition, didn't you?"

Dahlia nodded. "I'm surprised you didn't figure it out sooner."

Julie felt the realization sinking in. Just like that, Dahlia had paid that bill. That enormous bill. Dahlia, not her mother. *Not Mom. Mom didn't pay my tuition on the sly.* Julie was shocked—and hurt. "I thought my mother—Well, that it was her way of saying maybe it was okay that Matt and I got married. Even if my father didn't agree with her . . ."

Dahlia plopped down next to her and studied the floor. "Well, *I* believed in you guys," she said quietly. "I mean, I guess I was kind of jealous at first, but I think you and Matt are really made for each other. As corny as that sounds."

Julie was touched. "Look, I didn't mean for it to sound like I was mad at you. The opposite—totally. It's just . . ." She shook her head. Thousands and thousands of dollars. No matter how much Dahlia's family had, Julie couldn't take that kind of gift.

"Julie, you're my best friend in the whole world," Dahlia said. "It was either I paid or early graduation for you. I couldn't stand that you'd have to drop out. I mean, me—I'm not so great a student. Well, maybe a little more, now. But you needed to stay in school. Anyway, I know the pressure you guys have been under. I just wanted to help."

"I don't know what to say." Dahlia was a real friend. Julie suddenly felt like crying. This on top of everything else. Why did life hit such highs and such lows—and sometimes both at the exact same time? "I promise, we'll figure out a way of paying you back." She fought the lump in her throat.

"You don't owe me a thing," Dahlia insisted. "Except to keep being my friend."

Julie threw her arms around Dahlia and gave her a hug. "You're the best, and we *will* pay you back."

Dahlia hugged her back. "Why couldn't I get another roommate like you?"

Julie smiled. "Yeah, I've got to admit, it is a little different around here than it used to be." She glanced through the open door into the outside room of the divided double. Cindi was off somewhere, but traces of her filled the room—hanging crystals that threw little rainbows all over her walls, posters of forests and seacoasts with sappy poems under them, stuffed animals everywhere: a seal, a lion cub, a whole family of fuzzy dolphins.

"She makes me want to go off and kill some whales," Dahlia said.

"Dahlia!" Julie said, trying not to laugh.

"Kidding, just kidding." Dahlia put her hands up. "I love whales, too. I just hate her."

"Well, at least she's not costing you anything," Julie joked back.

"Only my sanity."

Julie grinned. But she was filled with surprise and confusion over Dahlia's "little" present. "Hey, Dahlia, what did your father say when he found out? I mean, it's a lot of money. Didn't he freak a little bit?"

Dahlia started to blush. "Well, actually he doesn't know about it."

"I don't get it."

"Look, don't go blabbing it around, Julie. But that money came out of my own account. I doubt my parents will ever know."

"Wow. You're amazing." Julie couldn't mask her surprise. "Hey, I know you're not royalty or anything, but if you don't mind my asking, just how rich are you?"

Dahlia's face grew serious. "Well, you know that list that comes out every year of the ten richest people in the world?"

Julie stared at Dahlia with huge eyes. She couldn't help it. Ten richest? In the whole world?

"Well, I'm not on that list. And neither is my father," Dahlia said, breaking into laughter. "Fooled you, though, didn't I?"

Julie laughed, too. "Well, there's always next year."

Seventeen

"If you want to take a handout, that's your business!" Matt exploded. Julie reeled at the anger in his voice—anger that seemed to be launched right at her. He sat up in his hospital bed, his fists clenched, his cheeks reddened with fury against his overly pale face.

"It's not like I asked her for it," Julie defended herself, her muscles clenched, her body tight in the stiff-backed chair by his bed. "It's not like I even knew anything about it."

"Doing something for the little people," Matt went on, ignoring her words. "Probably makes her feel less guilty about Daddy's millions."

"Matt!" Julie was stung by the meanness in his voice. "I feel weird about it, too, but for heaven's sake, she did it because she really cares about us! She wants to help."

"Help. Great. Let's everybody help poor, sick Matt who can't help himself," Matt muttered.

Julie felt her own anger rising. "Why is it so awful to have your friends care about you?"

Matt gave a contemptuous laugh. "Treating me like I'm helpless—you think that's caring?"

Julie looked at Matt in his metal-railed bed, the call button an arm's reach away. Lying there, weak and angry, he *was* helpless. Julie sighed with frustration. "Matt," she said more softly, "I told her that we'd consider it a loan."

Matt's expression didn't soften a bit.

"What other choice do we have, anyway?" Julie asked with resignation.

"Look, I'm going to be out of here in another week," Matt said. "Out of here and back at work."

Julie bit her lip. And what about two more weeks after that when he was back in the hospital again, not earning anything? Meanwhile, all those medical bills would be piling up. "Matt, we need her help. At least right now."

Matt glared at her. Julie could feel the strength of his anger, his frustration. And his fear. She looked into his gray eyes and she could see it glimmering there—the fear he was working so hard to keep inside, the fear he biked away or ran away, the fear he held in check by insisting he could do it all himself.

Why couldn't he just let it out? Why couldn't he open up to the people who cared about him the most? Julie felt the coldness of his gaze.

And then she saw it disappear. A smile began at the corners of his mouth. She smiled back.

But he wasn't looking at her. He was looking past her, behind her. "Hey, my main man!" he called out.

Julie turned in her chair to see Danny coming into the room, walking slowly, a Cubs cap on his bald head. He looked thinner than ever, with deep, dark circles under his eyes, but his hand was raised in a victory fist. "I walked ten times around the whole floor," he said triumphantly.

"All right! That's what I like to hear," Matt said. "We'll have you back to running bases in no time."

Danny's swollen face lit up in a smile. "You think so? Hi, Julie!"

"Hi, Danny," Julie said.

"Hey, when we get out of here—when we're better," Matt said to Danny, "we're going to go out to the ball field and stuff ourselves full of hot dogs and popcorn."

Danny smiled even wider. "Really?" He came over and sat down on the edge of Matt's bed.

It was impossible for Julie not to be moved

by the tenderness between them. "Sounds great," she put in.

Matt didn't even look at her. He leaned forward and gave Danny a gentle sock on the arm. "Just the two of us, Champ, what do you say?"

Julie felt a stab of hurt.

"Oh, guess who you missed when you were out walking around?" Matt went on talking to Danny. He made an exaggerated scowl and crossed his arms over his chest.

Danny giggled. "Nurse Rodriguez!"

Matt nodded. "I told her you'd be so sorry to have missed her. Should we ring the bell and tell her you're back?" Matt positioned his hand over the call button.

"No!" Danny protested, giggling even harder.

"Hey, and who's this?" Matt asked. "And how are we feeling this afternoon?" he said in a high, wobbly, sugarcoated voice. "My, I think we're looking better. Are we ready for lunch yet?"

"Nurse Johnson!" Danny laughed. "She's about three hundred years old," he said to Julie.

Matt and Danny continued to joke about the staff, about other patients in the hospital, about the hospital rules. Julie tried hard to include herself, laughing at the right places, and nodding at Danny's explanations to her about this person or that one. But Matt was freezing her right out. Why was he so angry at her? And at Dahlia and everyone else who wasn't sick? Why did he have to turn his back on them?

Julie's throat was tight, and her smile felt brittle. She stood up. "Well," she said softly, afraid she might start to cry, "maybe I should go."

Matt glanced up at her. "Fine," he said.

She leaned down and gave him an awkward kiss on the cheek. "Julie?" he whispered.

Julie felt a ray of hope. "Yeah?"

"Tell Dahlia to spend the money on someone else."

"You tell her," Julie retorted.

Translate: If I had known, I would have tried to help. Julie read to herself from her French grammar book. *Si je savais*— Or was it *si j'avais su*? The thought of Matt's cold gaze and hard words made it impossible to keep her mind on her work.

She leaned back in the chair of her library study carrel. She had thought she and Matt would fight this thing together. Together, in sickness and in health. But Matt was so determined to stand on his own two feet that he was pushing her away. Julie was angry. And on top of that, she felt guilty for being angry. Matt needed her. More than ever. But what could she do when he refused to admit it? Maybe he *should* have gone back to Philadelphia. Maybe his father could have taken better care of him than she could. She felt the tears welling up in the corners of her eyes.

The truth was, Julie could have used some babying from her own parents. But the brief moment of warmth she'd shared with her mother on the telephone had only reminded her of how far apart her family had grown. The person who'd really been there for her since she'd left home was Matt.

"Julie?" a familiar voice said.

"Nick!" Julie looked up at him, quickly wiping her eyes with the corner of her sweater.

"Are you okay?" Nick squatted down next to where she sat, concern etched on his fine features and in his green eyes.

Julie gulped and nodded, but her tears wouldn't stop.

"What's the matter? Is Matt—has something happened?" A note of cold fear crept into Nick's voice.

Julie shook her head. "He's okay," she said, sniffling. "I mean, he's not okay, but he's not any worse."

Nick nodded grimly. "That's good. I guess. So . . . ?" he asked gently, putting a hand on her shoulder.

Julie shrugged. "It's just that I don't know

what to do about the guy. I want to be there for him, but he doesn't want to be taken care of."

Nick gave a short, unhappy laugh. "I kind of got that feeling when I bumped into you guys at the movies."

Julie felt a flush of embarrassment. "Yeah. Look, I'm sorry he was so mean to you."

Nick waved his hand. "Hey, the guy's sick of all the special treatment. I just came along at the wrong time and—well, I'm not his favorite person these days, anyway." He frowned. "But I miss him."

Julie felt a cramp of sympathy—and a beat of frustration at Matt. Wouldn't it be so much easier if he let people in? "Nick, if it's any consolation, he hasn't exactly been the friendliest to anyone." She thought about their fight over Dahlia and began to feel her eyes tearing up again.

"Everyone's so worried about Matt," Nick said softly. "I know it's really tough on you, too."

Nick's quiet warmth just made it harder for Julie to stop the flow of tears. They trickled down her cheeks. "I went to visit him yesterday and we had a fight . . ." Julie hesitated. On that night, so many months ago, she'd also been crying over Matt. Nick had been there to listen. She'd sought comfort in his arms. . . . An unwanted memory surfaced in her mind—the feel of Nick's lips on hers, so soft, so caring. She looked away from him.

"Julie, you can talk to me. I'm your friend," he said. "At least I used to be."

She looked back. Nick knew what she was thinking. They'd always had a real understanding. From their first conversation right here in the library. Nick was a good listener. "Yeah, I would like to talk." That night seemed like a long, long time ago. "You want to go for a soda at the Rath?"

Nick smiled. "Definitely." He stood up and stretched his legs.

Outside, the night was cold and cloudy. "So, what did you guys fight about?" Nick asked, zipping up his ski jacket as they walked the short distance to Walker Main and the Rathskeller, the campus pub.

"Well, see, Dahlia did something when Matt and I were first married. Only I didn't know she did it," Julie began.

"Dahlia? I've-been-to-Italy-three-times Dahlia? I'll bet this is going to be some story."

Julie felt a flicker of protectiveness. "Well, it is, but not the way you probably think. Give the girl a break! So she's traveled more than some of us."

Nick laughed. "To tell you the truth, it's actually kind of interesting to have someone in class with a firsthand opinion on the Sistine

Chapel. And the girl does have an opinion."

Julie held back a little smile.

"So what is it she did that you didn't know about?"

"Well," Julie said, "she paid my second-semester tuition. Secretly. And then she paid all the rest of our bills this last time Matt went into the hospital."

Nick stopped walking. "She did *what*?"

Julie grabbed his arm and got him going toward the Rath again. "Come on, it's cold out!" She filled Nick in on the whole story.

"I can't believe it." Nick pushed open the door to Walker Main, and Julie felt a blast of warm air. "Is this the same Dahlia I know?"

Julie arched an eyebrow at him. "I guess you don't know her very well."

They walked through the corridors of Walker to the entrance of the Rath. "When we were stuck overnight in that blizzard on the way home for fall break, she never said a thing!" Nick marveled.

He and Julie showed their Madison College IDs to the student hostess, and made their way to a table at the back. The Rath was a modest-sized dark room, with heavy wooden tables and booths. Groups of kids sat sipping sodas and cracking jokes.

"She didn't tell anything to anyone. She was too afraid I'd find out and think I owed her something." Julie raised her voice to be heard above the noise and voices in the Rath.

Nick's surprise was plain on his face. "Wow! That's incredibly generous."

"Yeah, but Matt doesn't think so." Julie explained how Dahlia's secret good deed had led to Matt's angry declaration of independence.

"Yeah, well, I guess I can see Matt's side, too. It must make him feel so helpless." Nick shook his head. "It's so hard on both of you."

"Yeah, well, I'm definitely feeling pretty helpless," Julie admitted. "It's like Matt wishes I would just disappear or something."

Nick shook his head. "No way! I don't buy that for a second. He's just angry and scared."

Julie nodded. "Even if he doesn't want to admit it."

As they talked, she felt her bleak mood lifting a bit. Nick said all the right things, but it wasn't just that. It felt good to have his friendship back. The conversation turned to other things—to classes and upcoming midterms, and the student who'd been put on probation for throwing a cream pie at one of his professors on a dare.

Long after they'd finished their sodas and their glasses had been cleared away, they sat and talked. If Matt had known, it would have made him even angrier. But Julie tried to ignore the pinch of guilt. She needed her friends as much as she'd ever needed them. If she couldn't turn to them for comfort and support, she couldn't turn to anybody.

Eighteen

A burst of warm sunlight on Matt's face brought him out of a deep sleep. His eyes flickered, taking in the brightness little by little.

The clock on his bedside table read four P.M. It was a beautiful afternoon. Outside, the hospital lawn was a sun-washed green. The sky was cloudless and as blue as he could remember. The perfect time of day during the perfect time of year.

Matt thought about all the things he could be doing if he weren't lying in bed. A motorcycle ride with Julie's arms wrapped tightly around his waist, fast and hard through the back roads of Ohio. Maybe they'd head toward Lake Erie and dare each other to take a dip in the chilly water. Or else he'd go mountain biking or running. This was the perfect weather for either.

But no. Not today. Spring was arriving, and Matt couldn't join in to welcome it. Good clean fun was off-limits to sick people. Matt grimaced as he inspected himself in his hospital bed. Pajamas and a robe in the middle of the afternoon—what a joke that was. He knew he looked pale and tired, even though he'd slept away half the afternoon.

He gazed enviously out the window at a pair of joggers working their way into the distance toward a row of giant oak trees that swayed in the breeze. He could run twice that fast, if they'd only let him. Frustration swelled inside him. He hadn't felt good for a second since his fight with Julie over Dahlia's little charity number.

Julie. Thinking of her only intensified Matt's frustration. It wasn't only the money thing. She just didn't understand what he was going through. Sure, she tried to be there for him. She said she was pulling for him all the way. But that was half the problem. All the pulling for him, all the hand-holding and worrying was exactly what he didn't want. It just made him feel that much more like a hopeless invalid.

Outside, the sun seemed to be getting brighter and more inviting, while here, inside the cancer ward, there was nothing but sickness and death. How could anybody get better in a place like this?

Matt looked over at Danny, who'd been sleeping since late morning. Sleep had consumed the little kid more and more each day. And while showing him how to grip a baseball to throw a curve, Matt had noticed how much frailer Danny had become just in the short time they'd known each other. It took all the enthusiasm and determination that filled his little body just to hold on to the baseball. The night before, Matt had heard him crying in his sleep. How could the world be so cruel?

Danny's hopes of the future kept getting postponed. Before long, there might not be any at all. Was that what was in store for Matt? After all the pain and toxic drugs?

Chemotherapy. Every day you were pumped full of poison, and afterward, it rendered your system that much more drained of its strength. It seemed almost as if it caused more harm than good. After a while, you weren't even sure which was the enemy—cancer or chemotherapy, or both.

As Matt stretched his arms and legs, he felt weak. But of course he would. He'd been confined to his bed. Like Danny, he was slowly wasting away. Was he supposed to just lie there, passively, until he died? Should he just smile and say thanks when people left him bouquets of flowers as if it was his funeral, or when someone paid his bills for him because he couldn't manage it himself?

He needed his strength back. He needed his will to return. But how could he get stronger when Dr. Zinn had refused him his exercise? What he'd give for a good hard run now.

Outside, the sun was begging him to come out. Well, if he couldn't go for a run, at least a little walk around the grounds. Dr. Zinn did say that was okay. Maybe it would help to lift his spirits a little.

Matt got out of bed and went over to his closet to get his street clothes. He reached for his sweater and then his pants. *Why bother,* he thought. He stepped into his sneakers and tied his robe closed. *Might as well wear what I've got on.*

"Hey, buddy, what's up?" a tired, soft voice called to him from the other bed as Matt reached for the door handle.

Matt looked over at Danny, who wore a sleepy, puzzled look on his face. "Hey, pal. Just going out for a little walk. How you feeling?"

"Okay," Danny said. "Hey, I was dreaming about pitching for the Cubs. And guess what, Matt? I was using the curveball you taught me. Those batters couldn't touch me."

"Great, Danny. Hey, I'll see you."

"Okay. Matt? Make sure you wake me up if

I'm still asleep when the game starts tonight, okay?"

"Sure, buddy," Matt said as he opened the door and started down the hall.

Once outside, Matt took in a giant breath of fresh air. Wow! What a relief. He blinked in the sunlight, a tickle of giddiness stealing over him almost immediately. He began to circle the manicured hospital grounds, working his legs, pumping his arms. It was working like a charm. He covered the path around the grounds once, then headed toward the oak trees that he'd seen from his window. Sunlight, daylight, fresh air, a fresh breeze—it felt wonderful being back in the world of the living.

As his step quickened, he felt his heart pumping. A fast walk became a light jog. Nothing strenuous. But the rhythm of his legs met the sound of his own breath in his ears. He felt a rush of pleasure. He picked up the pace. Full strides, harder and faster, until he felt himself working up to full speed.

Just a few minutes, he told himself. *No real exertion. Just a few moments of speed and freedom. Then I'll head back.*

He reached the main road and had to jog in place for a few seconds while traffic passed him. His chest began to feel a little heavy. Nothing serious; he was out of shape, that was all. He crossed the road and started up a small hill. He felt a slight cramp below his stomach, and his arms and legs grew wobbly. *Fight it,* he told himself. *It will go away.* He pushed ahead, farther up the hill into the afternoon breeze.

There was a high-pitched ringing in his ears, and his stomach cramp worsened. Matt clutched his gut and tried to squeeze out the pain. The ringing grew louder still. His knees buckled. Matt felt himself falling, crashing to the ground. And then, black.

Matt's eyes were closed. Every few minutes they'd flicker slightly, as if they were about to open up, but then they'd droop shut again. His forehead and bald scalp were beaded with sweat. I.V. tubes ran from above his bed to the needles inserted in his arms. Another tube ran out of his nose to an oxygen tank. He moaned softly.

"Matt?" Julie whispered. "Matt!" Was he coming around? Could he hear her? He moaned again, but his eyes didn't open any farther. "It's all right, sweetheart." Julie fought to keep the panic out of her voice, to make her words soothing, lulling. She held on to Matt's limp hand. "I'm with you. I love you, Matt."

Dr. Zinn had told her that Matt's ambitious run had brought on a dangerous attack of pneumonia. Unconscious and in obvious pain, he was fighting for his life. Julie tried to picture all the love she felt flowing from deep inside her, down her arm, through her hand, and into Matt, like a white healing light. "Stay with me," she whispered. "I need you."

She thought she could feel her blood racing wildly through her veins. Her breath came fast and shallow and frightened. Her throat was dry and raw. She couldn't even cry. But she had to pull herself together for Matt.

"They say people can hear you, even when they're like that," Danny had said bravely, when he'd come to visit Matt in intensive care. "You've got to keep talking to him."

Julie thought about Danny. What must it be like for him to see Matt like this? How could he help but imagine himself growing just as sick? A ten-year-old boy on the brink of death. Danny was looking weaker and sicker every time Julie saw him. But he wasn't willing to give up. Not on himself and not on Matt. Julie took his advice.

"Remember the day we got married?" she asked Matt softly. She squeezed his hand. There was no response, but she continued talking. "Do you remember how sweet that room smelled, with the sun pouring in on all that wood? And the sound of the brook outside? I was so happy. It was so perfect. To have and to hold. For all the days of our lives. All the days, and there are going to be lots. I know it."

Strong, convincing, tender. She had to make Matt believe it. But deep inside, she felt a terrifying doubt about her own words.

Even if Matt didn't feel her hand, she couldn't let go of him. She wouldn't let go of him. He had to come out of this. He had to pull through. Matt. *Matt.* He didn't even look like himself. With her free hand, Julie took a tissue and gently wiped his brow. His face was at once bloated from the chemo and wasted by all the weight he'd lost. His eyes seemed to disappear into the dark bags beneath them. Matt. Always so strong and healthy and full of life.

"Hey, they say the weather's going to turn nice," Julie said to him. "Perfect for bike riding. Remember you said you wanted to show me that old abandoned house you found out in the woods? Well, I'm ready. I want to see it. You've got to get better soon, Matt."

She gave a start as she felt a hand on her shoulder. She let go of Matt's hand and whirled around. Julie found herself looking up at her mother. "Mom!" Behind her mother stood Tommy, holding a giant bouquet of yellow and purple flowers, and at arm's distance from him, stiff and solemn, was her father!

Julie half rose from her chair, and without quite knowing how, was suddenly in her mother's arms. Finally! After so long. She felt a welcome rush of comfort—followed by a moment of despair. Her mother's arms were around her because Matt might die. A sob racked her body. Her mother held her tightly. The tears flowed fast and hard.

Julie buried her head on her mother's chest. All the fear and pain was flowing out of her. She abandoned all emotion to her mother's care, like a child.

And then Tommy was hugging her, too, the perfume of the flowers enveloping them like a cloud. Julie gave her brother a huge squeeze. Without letting go, she looked over at her father. "Dad," she said through the tears.

He took several steps forward, and with shaky arms he embraced them all. "We're here, Angel. We're here." It was a nickname he hadn't used in a long, long time.

Nineteen

Marion sat at a small corner table in the library. The space in front of her was cluttered with medical textbooks about cancer, chemotherapy, and Hodgkin's disease. She'd spent the entire afternoon and most of the evening reading and taking notes, trying to better understand the illness that was threatening Matt's life.

"Find anything?" Fred asked, his voice soft and considerate.

"Shhh," she said, not picking her head up from her book. Marion knew she was being a little hard on him. He'd been sitting by her side all day while she studied. He'd breezed through his homework and about a half-dozen science magazines, but he'd spent a lot of the time just sitting, watching her, as patiently as he could.

But Marion had plenty more to read. Matt had

been doing so well until a few days ago. From everything she'd read, he was a prime candidate for a full recovery. But the look on Julie's face before she'd left for the hospital yesterday said otherwise. Matt was in really bad shape. Marion searched through text after text, trying to find any information about pneumonia and cancer patients. It had to be in one of these books.

"Hey, sweetheart," Fred tried again. "Can't I at least help you look?"

Marion sighed. "I just wish I could understand it, that's all."

Fred leaned over and planted a soft kiss on her cheek. It felt nice. "You know, Matt's doctor is one of the best. He must know a lot more than what's in those books."

"I know. But I keep thinking maybe there's something here."

"Like what, sweetheart?" Fred asked.

"I don't know." She shrugged. "Something." Marion reached for another book, *Cancer-Related Diseases,* and went straight for the index, hoping to find pneumonia.

She felt Fred's warm breath on the back of her neck. "He's really getting the best care, Marion." Fred kissed her again on the cheek, and then on her temple.

"Fred, please," she said, pushing him away. She frowned, finding no listing of pneumonia in the index.

"You don't care about me anymore. Is that it?"

Marion could sense the hurt in his voice. "That's not true, Fred."

"Then what's wrong?"

"I'm just really shaken up about Matt, that's all."

Fred shook his head. "There's something else, I can tell. It's me, isn't it? You're unhappy with something."

There was an awful moment of silence. Being in the library only highlighted the quiet. Marion could hear a girl writing over at the next table. She could practically hear another boy reading.

It was painful looking at Fred, his eyes so filled with worry, his fingers quivering with nervousness. He knew—and she knew—that there was something wrong. The problem was, Marion didn't know exactly what it was. She just looked up at him, wordlessly, and returned the worried gaze.

"If there's something you don't like about me, Marion, I could change it. Is it the way I dress? I know I'm not a prince of fashion."

Marion shook her head. "No, I love the way you dress." Fred dressed simply and casually. He looked great in jeans and plaid shirts. Maybe it was a little weird that he wore sneakers all through the winter. But all in all, he dressed fine, and without his Cincinnati Reds cap pulled down low over his red curly hair, he just wouldn't be Fred.

"Then it's the way I smell. Do I have bad breath?" He blew a breath on his own hand and sniffed.

Marion sighed. "No, Fred. Everything about you smells sweet."

"You think I'm ugly," he said with a pout.

"I do not. You're handsome, Fred." That was what had first attracted her to him. His soft red curls, his dimply smile, and the fact that he wasn't two feet taller than she was, as a lot of guys were. She wouldn't trade Fred's looks for anything.

Fred leaned close and whispered in her ear. "Don't I kiss well?"

"Fred! Don't be silly," Marion exclaimed.

There was a host of "shhhs" and "quiets" from some of the other students in the library.

Marion blushed. "I love your kisses," she whispered back.

Fred shrugged his shoulders, mouthing the words "What, then?"

"I don't know," she said. "Maybe it just gets like this after a while. You know, some of the specialness wears off a little after we get to know each other so well."

Fred looked as if he'd just lost his best friend. "That's not true of lots of couples. Like Matt and Julie, for instance."

"They have their problems," Marion said. "Remember a few months ago when Matt almost went back to Philadelphia?"

"Yeah, but still, they're always there for each other. Like now. Julie's been there with Matt practically nonstop for days."

Marion was quickly reminded of Matt's condition. She'd knocked on Dahlia's door this morning, and Dahlia had said that Matt was still unconscious. Marion wished she could help. "I just wish there was something, anything I could do." She sighed.

"Marion, we were talking about us, remember?"

She shrugged. "I don't know, Fred. We're just not the same as they are. They're married. They're in love. Like you said, Fred, Matt and Julie are there for each other. Always. I guess that's what love is all about. I mean, we—" She hesitated. The words came out so easily when she was talking about Matt and Julie. But she couldn't say them about her and Fred. "I guess we're taking things a little too fast, Fred."

Fred's head hung low. Marion didn't want to hurt him. She did lo—like him. A lot. He was her first real boyfriend. And the sweetest one any girl could ask for. But love? Maybe she wasn't sure how it felt yet. Or maybe the spell was beginning to wear off and she just didn't know how to admit it.

* * *

The hospital cafeteria was clean and bright, the walls freshly painted, each a different, cheerful color. There were hanging plants, and the soft, soothing sounds of string instruments came from speakers on either side of the room. Someone had tried to make it a pleasant place. But it was impossible to forget where you were for a second. Patients in hospital dress sat at several tables, some with family members or friends. Doctors and nurses strode in and out, looking busy and tired. At a table in one corner, an old man sat by himself, weeping silently. Julie took a sip of her umpteenth cup of bitter coffee.

"Julie, sweetie, why don't you let your father drive you home? Relax, take a hot bath, and get a little sleep," her mother implored. "We'll call you if anything happens."

Julie shook her head. She'd been up all night, but she wasn't about to go home and try to sleep. She knew she wouldn't be able to. Besides, if Matt's condition changed at all, she wanted to be right there with him.

"Jerry?" Julie's father said to Mr. Collins. "Same offer. One of us could drive you back to your hotel room."

"Thanks, Tom, but I want to be near my son."

If, a few months earlier, anyone had told

Julie that they'd all be gathered together—her whole family and Mr. Collins—past problems cast aside, she would have welcomed the day. But now she felt little joy. True, her parents and Matt's father were finally making steps toward a long-overdue peace pact. But what had brought them together overshadowed any slender ray of happiness. Matt's father looked absolutely blank, afraid to let himself think or feel too deeply. Julie knew that expression—she'd seen it on her parents' faces two-and-a-half years ago, after Mary Beth had died.

Two-and-a-half years, and the pain was still razor sharp sometimes. Sometimes, she still felt that chill right through her, as if she'd never get warm again. As if any warmth had died with her sister. It couldn't happen again. No. She couldn't lose another person she loved so fiercely.

Across the table from her, her mother and father held hands. It wasn't something Julie saw them do very often, but now it was as if they were putting their strength together for what might lie ahead. Tommy sat punching the keys on his pocket video game, but Julie could tell he wasn't really playing.

It had been a long night's vigil. At about three o'clock in the morning Matt had mumbled something, tried to form some words, and the doctors thought he might be regaining consciousness. Julie's spirits had soared, only to plummet like a downed plane when Matt slipped further away from her again. Her mind was exhausted, drained, yet her body was racing. She was alternately gripped with fear and strangely emotionless, unable to believe that this was really happening.

She glanced around the table at the grim, silent faces. *Don't give up now,* she pleaded wordlessly. *Not when I need my family. Not when Matt needs you.* Her eyes met her father's, and she tried to read what he was feeling. Not long ago, he was still so angry about her marriage that he and Julie had barely been on speaking terms. Now her pain—and Matt's father's—had touched something deep inside him. How would he feel if Matt got better? *If?* What was she thinking? Julie pressed her lips together tightly.

"Julie," her father said, breaking the silence at the table, "he's in God's hands right now. Try to let go of your doubts. Let him be."

Let go? But Julie wanted Matt, here and now. With her.

"A storm inside you can't help Matt right now," her father went on. "He needs to feel peace and strength and calm. And we need that, too. All of us." His voice gathered power and conviction as he spoke. "God has magnificent gifts of healing. If we believe that, then Matt will feel our hope."

Julie felt herself touched, if not by her father's exact beliefs, at least by his tone. And when she thought about it, was it really so different from what Danny had been saying when he'd told Julie to talk to Matt? Or what Dr. Zinn had meant about having the right attitude? Matt needed the belief that he could make it. And Julie needed to help give him that.

She did something she hadn't done in many, many years. She closed her eyes and prayed.

Twenty

The campus snack bar was filled to its usual late-afternoon capacity, but Dahlia barely paid any attention to all the commotion. She sat alone in the far corner, ignoring the noisy tables of students. Julie had called at four o'clock in the morning from the hospital, desperate. Dahlia had lain in bed afterward for hours, tossing and turning, hoping for Matt—and frantic that she might never see him again.

Once upon a time, when she'd first met him, she would have happily wished him away. He'd ridden out to Madison in the middle of the night, and suddenly it wasn't Dahlia and Julie anymore—Julie and Dahlia, the best roommates on campus. Suddenly it was Mr. and Mrs. Matt. The wedding. The happy couple. The big news on campus, with Dahlia off to the side, like a bridal bouquet that had been flung away. But once she cooled off a bit, she'd started seeing how happy Julie was. And little by little, she and Matt had discovered each other's special qualities.

Now he was part of Dahlia's Madison family. She knew he hadn't been happy about the bills she'd paid, but she felt sure that after this whole mess was over, when he got better, he'd see that she'd done it because she cared about him and Julie. If he got better.

She took a sip of her coffee, which was now cold. She glanced at the clock on the wall. She'd been sitting there for nearly an hour in saddened silence. On the table in front of her were two unopened letters. One was from Liz, her friend from New York, who was going to school out in California. Dahlia didn't feel like reading about Liz's latest escapades on the West Coast. Or about her Hawaiian spring break with her new boyfriend. Liz was the star of her own little world, and it wasn't going to make Dahlia feel any better to read about it now.

The other letter was from her parents. What could they say that could possibly cheer her up? The last time they'd written, it was to tell Dahlia how dissatisfied they were with her first-semester grades. They saved the heavy stuff for letters; otherwise, it was usually just a phone call telling her they'd be gone for two weeks or asking her if she'd written to Grandfather Sussman lately. She stared at the envelope. She couldn't bear any more bad news.

On the other hand, she couldn't very well just throw it away—although she had considered it. She picked it up and ripped it open. Pee-yew. One sheet of overscented, monogrammed notepaper in her mother's handwriting. As Dahlia started reading, her heart sank. Money—what else would they be concerned about? Her parents lived and breathed it.

> *Your father and I were recently notified about the unusually large withdrawals you've been making. What's going on? We only hope that you aren't spending that money on drugs. We need to talk, Dahlia. We're very disappointed with you.*

Drugs? Didn't they know her a little better than that? Dahlia felt herself getting hot with anger.

She read on.

> *Until we square this away, we see no other choice but to freeze your account, effective immediately. Your father and I leave for the spring fashion shows in*

Paris tomorrow. Back on the fifteenth. We'll talk then.

If they needed to talk, why didn't they call her? Too busy, as usual. And what were they doing mucking around with her personal account? As far as Dahlia knew, that money was hers, not her parents'. Furiously, she crumpled the letter into a ball. They seemed to care so little, she'd never expected her parents to even bother to check up on her. Besides, what was it to them? The money she'd spent on Julie was like nickels and dimes to her parents.

Drugs? Yeah, right. Were they ever in for a shock when she told them how she'd used it to pay for Julie's tuition! She wondered if they might be a little understanding when she told them she'd helped out a guy who had cancer. A guy who might die.

An uncontrollable trickle of tears began to work its way down her face. Julie had looked so scared when Dahlia had seen her a few days ago. Dahlia knew she hadn't been back from the hospital since Matt had collapsed. And last night, when Julie had called her, hysterical, there was nothing Dahlia could say to help cheer her up. Who cared about frozen bank accounts when Matt was fighting for his life?

"Hope it's nothing *I* said," said a friendly voice standing above her.

Dahlia looked up. It was Nick. She wiped away the tears. "Hi."

"What's the matter?" he asked.

She shrugged. "It's Matt."

Nick froze. "Oh, my God—"

"No, it's not that," she said. "He's still hanging in there."

There was a moment of temporary relief. Then a look of deep worry on his face. "What, then?" he asked.

Dahlia told him about the recent turn of events.

Nick slumped down in the chair next to her. He kneaded his forehead with his fingers, the frustration, confusion, and helplessness showing. "I've been so busy with a paper, I didn't even call Julie this week. I'm the worst friend," he lamented.

"It's not your fault, Nick," Dahlia said.

"Man, this is awful. I've got to do something. What can I do?" There was an almost hysterical edge to his voice.

Dahlia shrugged. "Just hope. It's about all any of us can do now."

They sat in silence for a while. Nick was fighting to hold back tears of his own. "I'm really scared," he said.

"Me, too." Dahlia could feel her voice trembling. She knew she looked horrible, too. She realized that she was wearing an old sweatshirt and a pair of blue jeans. She'd just thrown them on without thinking this morning. Too depressed even to care about how she looked. "I'm a total mess." She buried her head in her hands and felt a rush of tears.

"It's going to be all right," Nick said. Dahlia felt his hand on her shoulder. Strong, soothing. It felt nice, and it felt like it belonged there.

She shook her head. "They don't know that he's going to be all right. He's in intensive care right now." The tears came faster and harder.

She felt Nick circle his arms around her. "Hey, it's okay," he whispered. "It's going to be okay." But his voice was wavering out of control. Dahlia looked up at him. His green eyes were glossed with tears. They held each other's gaze, sharing their compassion as well as fear. Nick didn't look away.

Dahlia was filled with a strange mixture of warmth and sadness. Her heart beat wildly. She could feel Nick's heart pounding, too. She reached up and returned his hug. He drew her even closer. She needed his strength. She held him with all of hers. In a shared caress, they shed their tears for Matt.

Dahlia felt Nick's hand gently stroking the side of her face. "It's okay, Dahlia. I know it's going to be okay." He kissed the top of her head, slowly, lingeringly. Dahlia tipped her face up toward his. His lips found hers. His mouth was soft and warm. Dahlia could taste the salt from their tears that continued down their faces.

She could hardly believe what was happening. It felt strange, and at the same time, wonderful—a mixture of sadness and affection. They kissed for a long time, gently probing, riding the swell of powerful emotions. Time and space seemed to melt away. Nick's arms remained wrapped around Dahlia. She could feel his tenderness and hope—and fear. She let her head fall against his chest. She lay there, sobbing, finding solace in Nick's nearness.

"Matt? Can you hear me? Matt?"

Out of the blackness, a voice. Where was it coming from? Matt fought his way through a dark, cold fog to get to it.

"Matt? Sweetie? I love you."

Who was calling him? The voice seemed so far away. Matt struggled. He felt so alone.

"I'm still here for you. I'm going to wait here till you open up your eyes. I know you're there, Matt. I love you."

He heard it again. Suddenly, he felt something. Someone was touching him—holding his hand and stroking his face. It felt good. Yes, he knew that touch, and he knew that voice, too.

"Julie?" he called out into the dark. "Julie!"

"Matt, it's me. I'm right here!"

He felt her hand squeezing his. Light flickered behind his closed, heavy eyelids. And then the world slowly began to appear. He worked to open his eyes. He was met with a burst of white light. He blinked. And there she was, dark hair, the wide eyes, the soft, round face—Julie.

"Julie." His throat pulsed with pain, and he could barely talk. "I heard your voice calling me."

"Shhh, Matt, shhh. Oh, thank God, you're okay." She brought his hand to her warm, soft lips. "I knew you were listening. Welcome back, Matt."

"Nice to be back," he said in a croaking whisper. He brought his hand to his face. There was a tube running out of his nose. "I think. Where've I been?"

"Look who decided to wake up." A nurse he'd never seen before was suddenly holding his arm and taking his pulse. "Can you wiggle your toes, Mr. Collins?" she asked.

"Ow!" He could wiggle them, but moving his legs hurt tremendously. In fact, everything was sore. His eyes were still struggling to adjust to the light of day. Matt felt as if he'd been in darkness for a long time. As his surroundings came into focus, he realized he wasn't in his own room. This one was a lot bigger. There were at least a half-dozen other beds, and lots of machinery. There were vases filled with flowers on the table next to him, a potted plant, some get-well cards, and a fruit basket. It looked sort of like somebody had just died—or was about to.

"What's going on? Where am I?" he asked, forcing the words out. "My throat— It hurts to breathe." When he moved his free hand toward his throat, he noticed two more tubes hooked into his arm.

"Take it easy. Try to relax," the nurse said.

"Jules?" He needed an explanation.

"Do you remember anything? Leaving the hospital to go for a run?"

Matt tried to think through the fog in his head. But the darkness was all he could remember. Leaving the hospital . . . Leaving the— Yes. Suddenly he could remember. Running outside, all that sunshine. It felt so great. He remembered running hard up a hill. But then what?

As Julie explained what had happened, Dr. Zinn's voice came into Matt's head. *You can't argue with the figures. Your blood count's too low.*

"Three days? I've just lost three days of my life?" He started to shake his head, but it hurt too much. No wonder he felt like this.

"Stay still," the nurse told him.

"Squeeze my hand, Jules," Matt said.

A look of panic showed on her face. "I am squeezing it. Can't you feel it, Matt?"

Matt smiled. "Of course I can," he said

through the pain in his throat and lungs. "That's why I want you to squeeze it harder." There were tears beginning to roll down Julie's face.

"Tears of joy, I hope," Matt said.

Julie nodded. "I was so worried. You don't know what you put us through."

"Us? Who's us?"

"Everyone," she said. "I guess I should warn you, Matt. All of Philadelphia came out to see you. My family and your dad are here."

All of them, here? The severity of his situation was beginning to sink in. "Came to see me die, huh?" he asked, motioning toward the floral arrangements.

"They came because they care about you. Because they love you, Matt."

He could hear the nurse talking on the wall phone behind his bed. "Mr. Collins has regained consciousness. Signs are very good. Very responsive. Could you page his doctor, please?"

"They really all came out?" Matt asked. "What happened between our folks? I'm not sorry I slept through the fireworks."

"Actually, it wasn't like that at all," Julie said, smiling. "Everybody's been on their best behavior."

"It's just an act, I'm sure," Matt said. "You know, until I—"

"Matt, stop it!" Julie insisted. "Don't think that way. And it's not an act. I think they've all seen how much we mean to each other. And they're beginning to accept it. Really."

As if on cue, Matt looked toward the door and saw them all on their way toward him. Led by Julie's brother, Tommy, and Danny, they came eagerly to his bedside. Reverend and Mrs. Miller stepped to one side to let his father rush forward. Matt looked into his father's face. He had never seen him so full of fear. He came to the head of the bed and then stood there, frozen, unable to speak.

"Hey, all right!" Tommy was shouting. "I knew you'd wake up!"

"Hey, Matt," Danny said. "Now we can watch the basketball game tonight. The playoffs start, you know. Tommy, you can watch with us, too."

Matt turned from his father to the boys. Danny and Tommy had obviously become fast friends. They stood next to each other, smiling. He noticed how different the two kids looked, even though they were almost the same age. Julie's brother towered over Danny. Health versus sickness, it was all glaringly clear.

Julie's mother held a crumpled handkerchief. Reverend Miller's hand rested on her back. Even Julie's father, the Reverend Miller, who Matt had always feared hated him, looked happy to see that Matt had regained consciousness. Matt's eyes scanned them all, and came to rest on his father again. His dad's eyes didn't waver from Matt's face for a second.

"Hi, everyone," Matt said. "Hi, Dad."

"Son, I—I—thank God you pulled through. How do you feel? I've been so worried." He let out a major sigh of relief. "Thank God," he said again, glancing over at Julie's father.

"We all knew you'd stay with us, Matt," Mrs. Miller said.

Julie's father took a step closer. "Matt, you've given our daughter—well, all of us—quite a scare. But now you've answered all our prayers."

Matt wasn't quite sure what to say. Julie's family, his father, everyone seemed so dramatic. Was it really that bad? "You know what? I'm hungry. In fact, I'm starving!" he said. His eyes moved to the I.V. "Is this what I've been eating for the past three days? You know, every time they put me on an I.V., they always try to convince me it's like a bacon-and-eggs substitute, and I always tell them they're totally crazy."

Smiles at last.

"Well, I don't know about food with those tubes in you," his father said. "But here's your doctor now."

Matt looked toward the doorway and saw

Dr. Zinn walking in. He wore the same serious expression that Matt remembered on him the last time he'd seen him.

"Hey, Doctor, Matt says he's real hungry. Can we go get him a sandwich?" Tommy asked.

"Tommy, please," Mrs. Miller said, grabbing hold of him.

"Can't he have something to eat?" Tommy persisted.

"Whoa! Slow down," the doctor said. "Well, Matt. You gave us quite a scare."

"So I hear," Matt said. He paid particular attention to his doctor's face, trying to get some sort of idea of how serious his condition really was. Dr. Zinn wore a slight smile, a professional, neutral sort of smile. "How are you feeling, Matt?" he asked.

"Okay. A little weirded out. Sore. This tube in my nose is awful."

"He's hungry," Tommy whispered to his mother.

"Tommy, that's enough," Reverend Miller said.

"Okay, everyone. Sorry, but visiting hours are over. Matt is going to need peace and quiet for a little while. Julie, you can stay. The rest of you will have to wait till tomorrow to visit with him. And don't worry, young man," he said to Tommy. "I'll see to it that he gets a good hot meal, okay?"

"Yes, sir," Tommy said. "See you tomorrow, Matt."

"Are you sure I can't be of some help, Doctor?" Matt's father asked. "Anything. I could—"

"Mr. Collins," Dr. Zinn said, "I think it would be best if you went and got some rest, and came back to visit in the morning."

"Okay," he said. "Matt, I—I'm so glad you're all right." The emotion in his voice said more than the words.

"Dad," Matt said softly. "Thanks for being here."

His father suddenly bent down and kissed Matt's forehead. "I'll see you tomorrow, son."

As they all said good-bye, Matt could barely believe that his father exited with his arm on Mrs. Miller's shoulder.

"Nice family," Dr. Zinn commented.

Matt looked at Julie and gave a little wink. She winked back.

"Matt," the doctor said with a sigh. "I'm going to resist the major lecture. Rather, I'll welcome you back to the world of the living. You're going to need at least a couple of days' solid rest before we can continue with the chemo. Solid," he stressed, raising his eyebrows. "I think you know what I'm talking about, hmm?"

Matt nodded.

"When you're ready, we'll put you back on the protocol. Then you'll need another three days of chemo before we send you home this time. We've still got a fight ahead of us. Do you understand?"

Matt heard the deadly seriousness in his doctor's voice and a wave of fear crashed over him. "A fight . . ." he echoed.

"If you want to lick this thing—and I assume you do—you won't pull a stunt like that again," Dr. Zinn continued. "I'm putting Julie on patrol for now. I'll have them move you back to your room as soon as possible." He reached down and removed the tube that was hooked into Matt's nose. "What do you say, you want to breathe on your own from now on?"

Matt nodded.

"I'll see you tomorrow. Bye, Julie," he said as he headed for the door.

"I thought he said he was going to save the lecture," Matt said. "Sure sounded like one to me."

"He's on your side, Matt. You've got to listen to what he tells you."

"I suppose." Matt reached for Julie's hand. The softness of the touch helped to unleash a wave of emotion. Matt felt a flood of tears coming on. "Jules? I'm scared."

"Me, too," she said, bringing Matt's hand up to brush against her own tear-stained face.

Twenty-one

Julie took one last nervous glance around to make sure the apartment looked okay. She'd straightened and cleaned, and splurged on fresh tulips that she'd set in a vase on the small side table in the living room. Outside the windows, the sky was just beginning to darken over the town green. Julie switched the radio on softly to a classical station. The music of a string quartet filled the room.

Home. Except that with Matt not here, with Matt lying so sick in his hospital bed, it didn't feel very homey. Julie bit her bottom lip. Over the year, things had been so rocky with her parents that she'd begun to think they'd never come visit her in the little apartment, her first home with Matt. And she'd certainly never dreamed of the awful circumstances that would finally bring them here. A home without half of what made it a home.

Julie looked at the clock on the kitchen wall. Her parents and Tommy would be arriving any moment. Now that Matt was out of intensive care, they were checking out of their hotel near the hospital, saying good-bye to him, and coming to take Julie out to dinner before they flew back to Philadelphia. Back to work, to school, back to their lives at home.

And Julie would go back to classes, back to her job. . . back to waiting for Matt to get better. It seemed as if that was all she'd done since Matt had gotten sick. Wait for Matt's test results. Wait for Matt to come home from the hospital. Wait for Matt to regain consciousness. Wait for his condition to improve. Wait with her fingers crossed, and her breath held, hoping she wasn't waiting in vain.

Julie plopped down on the sofa. She was so tired. She had to stop thinking about Matt. Just for a few minutes, a few seconds. She picked up her newly typed journalism assignment, lying on her book bag at her feet. *Where Should Dogs Go? Here's the Scoop.*

She put it back down. Was there anything more meaningless in the world than this article? She could barely remember how she'd managed to get it done. The weeks since Matt's diagnosis had begun to blur together into one pointless nightmare. Her eyes stung with tears.

But as the doorbell sounded, she wiped them away quickly. She got up and pressed the buzzer Matt had installed. Footsteps filled the stairwell. Julie took a deep breath and tried for a cheerful expression. She opened her front door. "Hi, everybody," she said brightly.

As her mother, father, and Tommy came in, they each kissed her on the cheek. Her mother, the last to step inside, was carrying another bouquet of flowers—daisies and baby's breath. She held them out to Julie. "For your apartment."

"Thanks," Julie said, not adding that it was starting to look like Matt's hospital room in here. "So—how was he feeling?"

Her mother glanced around the living room. "Well, the doctor paid a visit while we were there, and he says Matt's ready to go back to his regular treatment," she said evenly.

"Really?" Julie began to smile. But she stopped as she noted the silent, unreadable look her parents exchanged. "Well, that's good, isn't it?"

"Yes, Julie," her father said. "Doctor Zinn said that Matt's blood count is out of the danger zone, and his body is strong enough for chemo. He ought to be a candidate for fast progress."

Ought to. But was he? Julie looked from her

parents to Tommy. Tommy lowered his gaze to the forest-green carpet. Julie felt a shiver of fear. Something was wrong. "Tommy, what?" she asked. She moved over and put a hand on her brother's arm.

Tommy shrugged. "The guy's totally wimping out," he said, his voice thick with hurt and anger. As he looked up at her, Julie saw a reflection of her own deepest fears. "The doctor told him all this good news," Tommy went on, "and it's like he didn't even listen. Danny was more psyched for him than he was."

"Tommy, shhh," her mother interjected. "Matt's been through more than any of us can imagine. He was just very tired. Julie, dear, why don't you show us around," she said, changing the subject abruptly.

Julie swallowed hard. "Sure. This is the living room. I guess that's obvious." She gave an unconvincing laugh.

"Very nice," her father said, his eyes going from the poster of Monet's *Water Lilies*, which had once hung on the wall of her dorm room, to Matt's mountain bike, leaning against the wall closest to the door, to the simple furniture they'd purchased secondhand. Julie noticed he avoided looking at the funky, leopard-print armchair that Dahlia had given them as a gift. Too wild for her father the reverend. If Matt had been here, they would have laughed about that afterward.

In the kitchen, she watched her mother take careful stock of the gleaming appliances, the dishes drying in the drainboard, the spice rack above the stove, the checked curtains. Then a look at the rest of the house. Her parents peered into the bedroom almost timidly. Julie had a moment of feeling as if she'd been caught red-handed as she followed their gaze to the queen-size bed. *Silly,* she told herself. *You're a married woman!* Besides, she thought morosely, she'd been sleeping in that bed by herself lately.

And then they were back out in the living room, standing around a bit awkwardly. "Well, it's lovely," her mother said.

"Yeah, cool! I can't wait till I have my own place," Tommy said, impressed.

"It reminds me a little of the place your father and I had, over the rectory at the church where he led his first congregation," her mother said. And then: "You've grown up so fast!"

Julie felt a funny rush of warmth toward her mother. Maybe Julie hadn't expected to grow up quite this fast, either. If anyone had told her a year ago that she'd be married with her own apartment by now, she would never have believed it. But any trace of humor vanished almost instantly. *Married and visiting my husband in the cancer ward.*

She noticed her father eyeing the pile of bills she'd stacked neatly on the coffee table. He looked over at her, then back at the bills. "So," he said, uncomfortably. "It must be hard to make ends meet."

Julie remembered his angry words just after she and Matt had gotten married: "You've made a choice to be on your own now." She looked at the pile of envelopes, too. Part of her wanted to tell her parents what Dahlia had done. Maybe now that she needed Mom and Dad so badly, they'd put aside their high principles and help out. But the peace with them was so new, so fragile. They hadn't even cemented it with words yet. Her parents had come out to be with Julie when she was frightened and alone. She was glad they were here. But they still hadn't discussed the problems between them, hadn't cleared the air and agreed to start anew.

She didn't feel ready to tell them how Dahlia had stepped in to help when they wouldn't. It would only make everyone more uncomfortable. This wasn't the time. Not now. Not when all her thoughts were concentrated on Matt.

"The bills are all paid," she said, trying not to sound guilty.

"I don't know how you do it," her mother said, awe and pride in her voice.

"We work hard," Julie said. "Dahlia—my old

roommate—she helps out sometimes." There was that urge to tell them the whole truth. But she couldn't. Not yet. "I mean, she gave us the TV, and the toaster oven, and a bunch of other stuff. Like that armchair." She sneaked a look at her father, who looked at the wild leopard-print chair with a solemn face. "Dahlia's really great. She's been totally incredible through—well, through everything with Matt. I wish you could have met her while you were here."

"Well, it wasn't the best of circumstances," her mother said gently. "Next time."

Julie nodded. Next time. She could only hope that next time would be happier. But what if it wasn't? In the past few terrifying days, with Matt fighting to hold on to a fine thread of life, Julie had looked his death in the face. He was out of danger now—for the moment, at least. But the fragility of his life remained impressed on Julie's mind—and in her heart.

She didn't want to be thinking this way. And yet Matt was thinking that way himself. Ever since he'd gone back into the hospital this last time, Julie had seen him sinking deeper and deeper into despair. Even Tommy knew it. How was Matt supposed to get better when he'd lost the will?

Julie's mother must have sensed the direction of her thoughts. "Perhaps we should make a move for dinner," she said.

Her father agreed. "We've got a plane to catch in a few hours. How about that Italian place we ate at when we brought you out here?"

Suddenly, Julie noticed Tommy staring hollowly in the direction of Matt's bicycle, as if reminded of the fact that he wasn't here to use it. "Great! Tommy, how many bowls of spaghetti are you packing away these days?" she said as cheerfully as she could. But she knew she wasn't fooling Tommy.

No one was going to have much of an appetite tonight.

Dahlia drained her second cup of coffee and left the snack bar for Fischer. Her class started in about five minutes. She didn't want to miss any of the lecture, but she was in no hurry to get there, either.

Dahlia sighed. The kiss had happened three whole days ago, and she hadn't seen Nick since. He hadn't stopped by, hadn't called, nothing. With any other guy, Dahlia would have called herself, but she'd been initiating the flirting with him all semester. He had to know that kiss meant something to her. Now it was his turn to make a move.

Dahlia hated to face the possibility that it had been a mistake—that the kiss was more an act of desperation over Matt than the beginning of something special. They'd both been so wound up that day. They'd both needed consolation and warmth.

Dahlia crossed Central Bowl, zigzagging around the students out on the grass despite the chill in the air. When people got so upset, they just did things they normally wouldn't do. She remembered the time she'd ended up spending the night with Paul Chase. If ever she'd made a major mistake, that was one. Even so, they'd shared a very tender night together. Still, it was something that shouldn't have happened.

As for Nick, Dahlia knew all about his history of kissing when he shouldn't. He'd done it with Julie, and before that, with his best friend from high school's girlfriend.

Dahlia pushed open the door to the Fischer building and headed up the stairs. Three days later, she could still feel Nick's lips. The warmth and tenderness of his kiss hadn't left her thoughts. As she exited the stairwell, there he was. Right there! They all but bumped smack into each other.

"Hi," she said, waving timidly. She took a half-step back. She knew the greeting was totally unlike her, but it was all she could manage. Besides, she definitely didn't want to come on strong.

"Dahlia, hi," Nick said. "How's it going?" He sounded happy to see her. "Uh—sorry I didn't stop by or anything. I've been sick all weekend. Weird stomach thing; I could barely get out of bed," he said.

"Oh." *Right. Sick in bed.*

"I did try to call you last night, but you weren't around."

"I was at the library." Dahlia shot him a questioning look. "You should have left a message."

"Yeah. I don't know, I never do too well with answering machines. I always seem to get flustered and sound like a total fool. Hey, I heard the great news about Matt. Julie called. Told me he was out of danger—well, you know what I mean."

"Yeah. No more pneumonia. But Matt's spirits are in the dumps. I just wish he'd get more psyched about getting better, the way he was at the beginning."

There was an awkward pause. Nick looked cute, that much was for sure. Clean shaven, nicely dressed in a pair of faded jeans, a cowboy shirt with pearl-studded buttons, and his black cowboy boots. Did he notice that Dahlia had spent a little extra time getting dressed this morning, too?

"Dahlia, before I chicken out— What do you say about you and me? A date, I mean. A real date. I know it sounds sort of corny and all, but we could go out for dinner or something."

Dahlia felt a wave of happiness enveloping her. "There's a great Italian restaurant right on Lake Erie. Julie and I drove there last semester and—" All of a sudden it hit her. She wouldn't be able to pay for dinner. She was practically broke until she cleared things up with her parents. "Oh, wow. I forgot. I seem to remember it being a little pricey. And, well, I'm sort of hurting for bucks these days. I know that sounds lame coming from me, but it's true. It's kind of a long story."

"Then we'll have something to talk about. How about I'll treat if you'll drive. Friday?"

"I'd love to," she said. She knew she couldn't hide the smile that was now covering her face. "I'm looking forward to it."

"Me, too," Nick said.

Dahlia wondered how she could wait that long. Why hadn't he said Tuesday? Or tonight, for that matter? On the other hand, she'd have plenty to look forward to this weekend. Nick was smiling ear-to-ear, his green eyes sparkling. She had the feeling he, too, was going to be wishing for Friday to come.

"Well, two of my favorite students. Good morning," Ms. Godarotti greeted them in her thick accent. "Such happy faces for two people who couldn't have more opposite viewpoints on the ceiling," she commented with raised eyebrows as she went inside.

Nick laughed. "That's another thing we'll have to talk about. Maybe I can talk some sense into you."

"I can't believe I've accepted a dinner invitation from the enemy," Dahlia said, winking. "And at an Italian restaurant, nonetheless. Well, maybe it'll be the right atmosphere to change your mind about a few things."

Twenty-two

"I just heard the good news, Matt. I bumped into Dr. Zinn down the hall, and he tells me you're ready to begin chemo again."

"Yeah, he told me," Matt said. His dad's face, like everybody else's, was filled with hope and promise at the news that Matt was ready to start again. They made it sound as if it were something to look forward to, like the seventh game of the World Series, or some sort of personal Super Bowl. As far as Matt was concerned, it was about the last thing in the world he wanted to do.

His father reached over and picked up a baseball glove that lay on Danny's bed. He held it in one hand—it was too small for him to put on—and punched his other hand into the palm of the mitt. "Where's your little friend?"

"Must be in treatment. If you stick around for a little while, you'll see what it's really all about, Dad."

His father punched at the glove again. "Remember the first time we ever played catch together?"

Matt stared past his father at the green wall across from the foot of his bed. "No, not really."

"Well, I do. It was on your fourth birthday. I got you a black glove autographed by Willie Mays."

"If you say so." Matt pulled the covers up under his chin.

"Cold?"

Matt shrugged. "A little."

"Hey, son, if it'll make you feel any better, I think he's really good. Your doctor. I'm sorry about all the pressure I put on you to come back to Philly. You were right. You belong here, Matt. With him and with Julie." He threw the glove back on Danny's bed.

Matt remained quiet. Why the apology now? It felt as if his father had come to say his final good-bye or something.

"Julie's a great girl, Matt. I've always thought so." He shifted his weight uncomfortably on the little wooden chair that was much too small for his large frame. "Son, I know you probably won't want to hear this, but your mother—she's worried sick about you."

"Not her again." She was the last person Matt wanted to think about now.

"She's phoned me every day to ask about you."

"You shouldn't have even told her, Dad," Matt said, his voice rising.

"Would a phone call or a simple letter be so hard? She's dying to hear from you, son," he said.

Dying. Way to go, Dad. "And now *I'm* supposed to call *her*? That's a joke, right? It might make more sense if it were the other way around, Dad. She's the one who should be calling me. Not that it would do any good."

"I know it's hard for you, Matt. But—"

"You're darned right it's hard! Don't you remember what she did? Dad, she split on us. On both of us! Packed her bags and ran away. Or have you forgotten? It probably didn't matter to you so much, since you had plenty of other—"

"That's enough, son," his father said sharply. He paused. "That was a long time ago."

"It sure was a long time ago. Like twelve years!" Matt exhaled heavily. "Twelve years, Dad, and hardly a word until this. Until her son's about to croak."

"Matt, don't talk like that," his dad said. "Your mother has tried to reach out to you. But you won't let her back in."

Matt let out a bitter laugh. "I don't even remember what she looks like. If she showed up, I wonder whether I'd even recognize her."

Matt saw that his father was struggling to keep from crying. "I know that she'd recognize you. In a second. She loves you, Matt. And I love you, too." Matt watched the tears begin to trickle down his father's face.

He felt a jolt of shock. Jerry Collins was crying. For the first time in his life, Matt watched his father cry. The tears looked awkward on his strong, rugged face. But it unleashed a wave of emotion in Matt. He felt his own tears welling up inside, struggling to get out.

"I love you, too, Dad. But Mom . . . Mom . . ." He choked on the word, burying his head in his hands. The tears came quickly and heavily. At first there was a soothing comfort to the salty flow, but he felt it give way to a sensation of emptiness and despair.

When he picked up his head his father was wiping his own eyes and blowing his nose into a handkerchief. "Son, you're all I've got in the whole world. I don't know what I'd do without you."

Matt never remembered seeing his dad so emotional. He'd always thought of him as Jerry Collins, Superman, always able to handle whatever came his way. The women were always crazy about him, and he'd always looked ten or fifteen years younger than he was. Even teary-eyed, though, Matt couldn't help but notice that his dad was still as strong and healthy-looking as always. In comparison, Matt felt every bit the invalid that he was. The dying son. It wasn't supposed to be this way.

"Look, Matt," his father said as he glanced at his watch. "I really should get going. My plane leaves in less than an hour. You know where to find me. If you need me for anything—"

Matt nodded. "I'll be fine, Dad."

"Matt? Don't shut me out, okay?" he asked, his eyes creased with pain and worry.

Matt looked away. But he knew his father's eyes were fixed on him. He felt a spark of guilt. He didn't want to push his father away, but it was too hard to look—he couldn't face this kind of good-bye, perhaps the last good-bye. He knew his dad was thinking the same thing. Matt wanted to reach for him, give him a big hug, but something inside was stopping him.

"When you pull yourself up and really beat this thing, beat it for good, I mean, you're going to really feel like a new man. You've got a long life ahead of you, son."

Matt shrugged.

"What do you say about all of us, you and Julie and me—we could all rent a place on the beach for a few weeks this summer. Sun, surf, lobsters, the whole bit on Cape Cod. It'll be a blast."

"I can't make any promises, Dad," Matt said flatly.

"I think you'll be around, Matt. I think you will." His father got up and headed for the door. He turned back, forcing a smile. "You got to try, huh?"

"So, it's just the two of us again," Julie said softly.

His head propped up on a pile of pillows, Matt scowled. "What, have you got Danny over there in his grave already? He may look ready for it, but he's just asleep."

Julie was stung. "Matt! I just meant all the parents are gone. That we get to spend a little time alone again."

"Yeah. Real quality time. This place is a total vacation."

Julie suppressed a surge of anger. She took a breath and tried again. "So, your dad must be home by now," she said. "Why did he take a plane, anyway? The way he drives, he could have gotten home faster by car," she added with a little laugh.

Matt gave a curt nod. Julie gritted her teeth. Okay, so it was a lame attempt at humor, but at least *she* was trying. "Well, it was nice to see him."

Matt shrugged. "Maybe."

They sat in silence for a while. Julie studied Matt's face. He glanced up at the blank TV screen, over at Danny, anywhere but at her. She bit her lip. She knew it was nothing she'd done—even if Matt acted as if it was. She just had to keep trying.

"Oh, listen, they're putting on a production of *Agamemnon* in Cleveland this spring—we're going to see it with my classics class."

"Oh."

"You remember that myth I was telling you about?"

"Sure," Matt said. "The one that started with that guy being served his grandchildren for dinner."

A whole sentence. Julie felt a spark of relief. Maybe Matt just needed to get off personal topics. Or maybe gruesome stories were about his speed these days—even if they were supposed to have taken place a couple of thousand years before his time. "Yeah, well, Agamemnon's several generations later, but he's still got the curse of the family on him. Anyway, I thought maybe you'd like to come with us to the play. Professor Blackburn says it's okay."

Matt wrinkled his brow. "I guess. If I'm around then." His voice went flat again.

"I already checked the dates. You'll be home then."

Matt gave a sharp laugh. "I meant around—period. Like around on the planet."

"Matt, I hardly think that's funny."

"I didn't mean it as a joke."

Julie felt her frustration boil over. "You're really a case! Can't you even try a little?"

Matt's expression went tight. "I tried. I tried so hard it put me into intensive care. Now I'm not going to try anymore. Look, I appreciate what you're doing—trying to get me up and stuff. I really do. But, Julie, I did everything right and it didn't work. I'm tired."

Julie knew what she should say. She should say, "I love you, Matt. I'm here for you, no matter what. I need you. I can't wait for us to be together, really together." But as she looked at Matt's face—swollen, his eyes dull—she felt as if she barely knew who he was anymore. Where was her husband and best friend? Where was the guy with so much courage and life and spirit? Was he ever going to come back?

She was numb. And she was tired, too. Too tired, even, to say the right words.

Outside his window, Matt noticed the same pair of joggers from last week. The sun shone, the trees swayed in the wind. But today, he had little desire to be out there. He felt drained from this morning's chemo treatment. Just moving was painful. Today was the worst ever. He had vomited practically nonstop from the moment the poison entered his system until an hour ago.

The flowers in his room that his visitors from Philly had brought him were beginning to wilt. *Like me,* Matt thought. He was so tired of staring at the sticky-sweet sympathy cards. It was too hard to keep up the positive attitude. He was losing the battle and soon he'd lose the war. Even Julie seemed to be pulling away lately, as if preparing herself for what was going to happen.

"He's been teaching me to throw curveballs. And how to swing through the pitch. It's for when I play with the Cubs!" Matt heard Danny's always chipper voice approaching. He pulled himself upright and forced a smile. But his smile vanished as Danny entered the room and Matt saw who was right behind him. Nick!

"He was going to leave all these great magazines at the desk for you," Danny said.

Nick gave Matt a nervous wave.

"I told him I was sure you'd want to see them right away, right, Matt?"

"Sure, buddy. Hi, Nick," Matt said flatly.

"Whoa, check out these bikes!" Danny shouted as he hopped onto Matt's bed, an open magazine in his hand. "Isn't this the one you said you wanted?"

He showed Matt the pictures. In fact, they featured the exact model Matt had dreamed of owning one day. A vintage Triumph, 1968, the best in the world.

Nick made his way cautiously from the door to Matt's bedside. "Dahlia told me you were coming home in a few days. Sounds great," he said, his voice bright and filled with enthusiasm.

Dahlia told him? The mention of her name made Matt go even colder. Dahlia, Miss Money, our Savior. And what was Nick doing talking to her anyway? As far as Matt knew, they were practically enemies. But why bother figuring it out? It wasn't worth getting all riled up about, anyway. He didn't even have the energy for it.

"I hope you don't have any of these magazines already. I tried looking for some of the more obscure ones. I found this whole stack at a tag sale not too far from my dorm the other day. Some biker dude was moving and he was unloading all this great stuff. I think I got there just in time, because this other guy was practically drooling over my purchase."

Matt leafed through a few pages. He had to admit it, it was pretty juicy stuff. Some of these magazines were rare classics. Matt was surprised the guy had sold them.

"Hey, he's not splitting town till next week

sometime. There might be some stuff left that you could use. I saw a couple of old helmets," Nick said.

"Yeah? What did they look like?" Matt asked, his curiosity piqued, despite how he felt about Nick.

"They were like these funky black bubbles, but they had this cool tinted green glass and a single stripe down the middle."

Matt flipped back to a page he'd just been looking at. "Like this, right?"

"Yeah, I think so."

"Wow! Vintage Honda. Nah, that would be too much. Who in their right mind would sell those?"

"I don't know, Matt," Nick said. "The guy seemed pretty strapped for cash."

"Yeah?" But suddenly Matt flopped back against his pillow. What good were a couple of vintage helmets if he might not be able to use them? And what was he doing yakking it up with Nick? On the other hand, these magazines were a lot more interesting than all the flowers and cards that only made Matt feel that much sicker. At least Nick knew what would cheer him up.

Matt felt a flicker of regret that he'd ever lost Nick's friendship. And he knew Nick was trying hard to put things right.

Matt thought about the kiss Nick and Julie

had shared, but the image of them together didn't come clear. Maybe it was everything Matt had gone through in the past months—that night seemed like a long time ago. With everything else he was dealing with, it was hard to feel much more than a fading soreness. Nick liked Julie. Understandable. He'd lost his head for a few moments. A few kisses. How long could Matt hold on to his anger?

Matt glanced down at the magazine picture again. "Stripe down the middle, huh? Yeah, well, maybe I'll look the guy up when I come home."

"He lives on Oak, right next door to that little white church."

"Sure. Well, thanks for the magazines, Nick."

Nick grinned. No somber face or tears. No dramatics. "Sure. Hey, I better be heading home. Maybe I'll see you around campus next week."

Nick gave Danny a little pat on the head and said good-bye. "Keep working on that curve, Danny. There's lots of competition out there."

Matt let out a hefty sigh. Maybe Nick wasn't the worst guy after all. And what *about* him and Julie?

Matt would be coming home in a few days,

only to return to the hospital two weeks later, that much closer to death. What then? What if Julie ended up alone—really alone? Matt had once been outraged at the idea of Julie and Nick together. But maybe it made sense, after all.

Twenty-three

Julie pressed her ears closed with her index fingers and tried to read. But the shouts and gunshots of the spaghetti western on the television cut right into her concentration. She slammed her French text shut and glanced over at Matt. He lay on the sofa with his arms crossed over his chest, staring blankly at the TV.

"Hey, Matt? It's so beautiful outside," she said, over the sound of the television. "Want to go for a little walk?"

Matt didn't even bother to look at her—or out the windows, where Julie could see the spring sun warming the tender shoots of grass on the town green. Voices and laughter floated up through the open window.

"Or how about going for a short run? Dr. Zinn said it's okay," she encouraged him. "In fact, it would be good for you, as long as you don't get into marathon mode."

Matt shrugged. "I'm watching TV."

Julie watched the cowboys on the screen galloping through Anytown, Wild West. Guns popping, dirt kicked up beneath their horses' hooves. Like every other western she'd ever seen. Matt had been home from the hospital for two days now, and he'd done nothing but lie prone in front of whatever program happened to be on. No amount of prodding seemed to be able to move him. If they'd had remote control, he wouldn't have budged at all.

Julie opened her French book again. *Conjugate each verb in the appropriate past tense,* she read. Past tense. Like, *Matt and I used to have a life. Once upon a time, my husband wasn't a couch potato.*

Julie sighed. The first couple of days Matt had been home, she'd tried her hardest—watching old movies with him, keeping up the conversation—both ends of it. She'd cooked his favorite meals, she'd tried everything. But Matt had refused to respond. Her own work was piling up. Besides, she deserved a life of her own, even if Matt seemed to have given up on his.

She pursed her lips. "So. Are you going to work tonight?" she asked, mentally crossing her fingers. *Please, let him do something, any-*

thing, besides lie there and lose hope.

Matt didn't take his eyes away from the screen. The cowboys rode off, and the dust cleared from Anytown. "I figure what's-his-face they hired has been doing just fine without me. Let him fill in for another night."

Julie felt her anger rising. "So you're just not going to bother?"

"Jeez, Julie, will you give me a break?" Matt was full of the kind of self-pity Julie had never seen in him, until his most recent stay in the hospital. "Look, if it's money you're worried about, Dahlia can just pay the rest of our bills. You wanted to take the handout—you ought to be happy." Julie opened her mouth to protest, but Matt cut her off. "Besides, it makes her feel good to spend her zillions on poor dying people like me."

Julie had heard enough. She jumped up from the armchair abruptly. Her head went light and dizzy, the room blurred around her, and she was seized by a wave of fury and nausea. She steadied herself with one hand against the chair, and waited for the feeling to pass. The room came back into focus, but her stomach remained queasy and anger still pulsed through her veins.

"I think I've heard about as much as I want to," she said angrily. "If you act like you're dying, pretty soon it's going to be the truth!"

She grabbed her book and stuffed it into her book bag, then strode over to the front closet and took out her jean jacket.

Matt shifted on the sofa to look at her. "Where are you going?"

Julie was halfway to the door, but something in Matt's voice stopped her—a note of pleading, something pathetic behind his words, as if he were a little boy who didn't want his parents to leave the house. Matt wouldn't let on that he needed her, but he didn't want her to go, either. A shimmer of sympathy went through her. But she shut it out as soon as she felt it. Why should she stay? To battle the sound of the television? To be the target for Matt's frustration and unhappiness? To watch him give up on everything that had once meant something to him?

She swallowed hard. "I'm going to the library. I've got work to do." She turned on her heel, left the apartment, and shut the door on Matt's misery.

Maybe it was the way they looked together that made the maître d' search for the most romantic table in the whole restaurant. Holding hands, looking out over Lake Erie, Dahlia even thought that it had been worth the wait.

She'd spent half the afternoon getting ready for their date. In the end, she'd chosen to wear something simple—simple but elegant. She had on a sleeveless black dress that hugged her body in just the right places. To accentuate the outfit, she wore a large pair of hammered silver and turquoise earrings and a thin antique silver necklace. She'd found them in the thrift shop below Julie's apartment and had impulsively spent her last dollars on them. After all, Nick was treating tonight, so she figured she'd splurge.

Nick must have been thinking along the same lines as Dahlia. He wore a cream-colored, soft cotton shirt and pleated, black wool pants with his favorite pair of cowboy boots. He'd gone southwestern, too, with a bolo tie and a silver clip that had been given to him as a present from a professor he'd met the year before on the archaeological dig in New Mexico. From the moment they'd sat down, they'd been making eyes at each other non-stop.

Candlelight, a white linen tablecloth, antique silverware, and crystal glasses, everything glistened. And the view out the window was spectacular. The shimmery, silver-blue water met a pale-lavender sky. Traces of fading burnt orange outlined a magnificent cloud formation on the horizon, as evening turned gradually to night. Dotting the water were the single lights from little fishing boats, the twinkle of lights from the harbor, and the blinking red dome of a lighthouse at the end of a distant jetty. Lake Erie, Ohio? Dahlia could swear that they'd been transplanted to Mediterranean Italy. Sexy, romantic—the mood was perfect.

In honor of Michelangelo and the Sistine Chapel, they'd tried to order in Italian. Nick had failed right from the start and had resorted to English. But Dahlia swore she could pull it off, after having been to Italy so many times with her family. Angelo, their waiter, had asked her to repeat herself three times, and with raised eyebrows, had let out a little snicker. Nick had sweetly told Dahlia that the waiter hadn't laughed *at* her, rather he had been laughing *with* her.

"At least I didn't say *chiaroscuro* or *impasto,*" she said.

It was as easy to enjoy each other tonight as it had been to fight with each other in the past. They'd talked nonstop on the drive to the restaurant, laughing about how much more fun it was to ride in Dahlia's car now that it was working. And from the moment they sat down at their table, their hands had been entwined.

Nick's green eyes got nicer the closer you got to them. Everything about him did—the sharp angles of his cheekbones and chin against the softness of his smile. His ears were at least two adorable shades redder than the rest of his face. Dahlia noticed a tiny little beauty mark that she'd never seen before, on the side of his neck. She knew she was only a short time away from getting to kiss it.

Sure, there was plenty to talk about. But sitting there in the warmth of the restaurant, looking and smiling at each other was about all either of them wanted to do.

"*Signor, signorina,* the antipasto." The waiter, dressed elegantly in black and white, placed the first course down before them. "*Buon appetito.* Happy eating," he said as he left them still gazing into each other's eyes.

Neither bothered with the food. Nick brought Dahlia's hands to his lips and kissed them tenderly.

"Hey," Dahlia whispered, "you know, you're awfully far away over there on the other side of the table. There's room for two on my side."

"You think our *signor* the waiter would mind? It might disturb the symmetry," Nick said.

"Let's try it." She smiled.

Nick took a quick peek to see if the waiter was watching, then swung around and sat in the chair next to Dahlia. "Mission accomplished. Now it's just the two of us, in a little corner." He touched his hand to her face and delicately stroked her cheek. Dahlia gave a little shiver as he found a sensitive spot. She felt herself melting to his touch. Nick drew closer to her and brought his lips to her forehead, letting them glide gently down to the bridge of her nose, the tip. Dahlia tilted her face up as their mouths met.

Everything felt so wonderful. Finally. As Dahlia drank in the happiness, she still found it hard to believe that these passionate lips were Nick's, the guy she'd nearly dumped on the side of the road in the middle of Pennsylvania. With each caress, the memories of that miserably cold night in the hotel room and the guy who once thought Dahlia was the biggest spoiled brat in the world faded away.

"Excuse me," the waiter said, clearing his throat. "*Signor, signorina. La pasta.*" He placed two plates of steaming pasta down next to the untouched first course. "I'll leave the antipasto for you for later, *sí?*"

"*Sí, signor. Molto grazie,*" Dahlia said with a big grin. She put her hand over her face to hide it from the waiter and stuck her tongue out at Nick. They both struggled to suppress their laughter. "The food looks delicious, but I think we may have overordered," she said. "What do you think? All of a sudden I'm not really very hungry."

Nick smiled. "Me neither. Leftovers might be delicious, though."

Dahlia nodded, falling right back into his arms. Their lips met again, as eagerly this time as before.

Twenty-four

Julie rolled over and stretched her arm out sleepily. Her hand fell flat on the rumpled sheets of Matt's side of the bed. She felt around. Nothing. The other side of bed was empty. She opened her eyes and propped herself up on one elbow. The blankets on the side where he slept were pushed down toward the foot of the bed, and Matt was nowhere in sight.

"Matt?" Julie called out, suppressing a yawn. No answer. "Honey?" She got out of bed, took down the bathrobe that was hanging on the back of the bedroom door, and put it on. Barefoot, she padded into the other room.

"Matt?" There was no one there. "Darn!" she said out loud. Matt had just sneaked out without even waking her up. She glanced around the living room. The bag he'd packed for the hospital was gone. She checked the front closet. His leather jacket was gone. His motorcycle helmet was, too.

No note, nothing. Julie wandered around the apartment, but she couldn't find even a little *see you* scribbled on something. She felt a queasy wave of anger. Sure, she knew Matt had to start his next cycle of chemo today, but he could have at least said good-bye before he'd left. Instead, he'd just gone, vanished, as if Julie didn't count for a thing.

She flopped down on the sofa. The queasiness didn't go away. Darn Matt! Darn him! He'd made the past two weeks almost unbearable, refusing to respond to anything anyone tried to do for him. Special meals, gifts, a funny story at the end of a day—Matt seemed to have no use for any of it. People had been calling—Marion, Dahlia, even Nick—but Matt wouldn't come to the phone.

Leon had finally just come by uninvited one afternoon, with his sax, to play Matt a new piece he was working on. Even that had hardly gotten through. Well, maybe a little. As the bright, golden sounds had filled the apartment, Matt had actually seemed to be listening, instead of just staring blankly into space or at a TV screen. But after Leon had left, Matt was even more sullen than ever, as if being brought into the world of the living was just too painful a reminder of what he stood to lose.

Julie frowned. Maybe she should be glad that Matt was out of here. Wait! Glad? What was she thinking? Matt was being stuck full of needles like a pincushion, pumped full of poisonous chemicals, and she was glad? She felt an overwhelming wave of guilt—and the queasiness in her stomach swelled into uncontrollable nausea. She tried to hold it down, but she could feel it in her belly, her chest, her throat. She jumped up and bolted for the bathroom, just in time to fling up the toilet seat and heave into the bowl.

She stayed there, kneeling on the cold tile floor, until she was certain she had finished. Then she rinsed her face, flushed the toilet, and drew herself a hot bath. She closed the toilet top and sat down as the tub was filling. It was the second day in a row that this had happened. Was it anger? Fear? Nerves? Some weird sort of sympathy for what Matt had been going through these past months? She was still queasy and she had an awful taste in her mouth.

She got up—slowly so as not to provoke another bout of vomiting—and picked up her toothbrush and toothpaste. The tube was flattened, empty. She tried to squeeze out a little bit more, then gave up and threw the old tube away. She opened the medicine cabinet. There was a new tube here, somewhere. Her eyes scanned the shelves. Baby powder, moisturizer, tampons.

She froze. Tampons. *Oh, my God.* How long had it been? One month, two months . . . with all the pressure she'd been under since Matt got sick, she simply hadn't kept track. But she was definitely late. No question about that. She sank down on the edge of the tub. The tiredness, the nausea! It couldn't be! She and Matt hadn't made love in so long. Not since before he'd started chemotherapy. The last time was the day, two-and-a-half months ago, when Matt had come home from Dr. Zinn's office and told her he had cancer. She remembered how they'd fallen into each other's arms. And made love. Desperate, passionate love—without using any birth control.

It was all beginning to make sense. Terrifying sense. Her husband was in a battle for his life, and she very well could be carrying their child!

Stupid, stupid, stupid, Julie chastised herself. She put the rectangular plastic dish containing her urine sample on the ledge of the bathtub. Next to it, she set up the little paper stand that came with the home test kit. She positioned the miniature test tube in the stand. How could she have been so dumb? If this test came out positive, she and Matt had no one to blame but themselves.

She thought about him, probably writhing in agony in the chemo room right now, or recovering, weak on his bed. He needed every last bit of strength just to get better. This couldn't be happening. Not now. Why hadn't they been more responsible?

It wasn't like either of them to be so careless. But then, they'd never come up against anything so frightening, so uncertain. They'd never before had to think about what it meant when they'd said "till death do us part." At the possibility of losing each other, their passion had ignited with such urgency that neither of them could resist it. It had been like quenching a devastating thirst. They couldn't stop even for a moment.

Now, Julie set her mouth grimly and followed the instructions that came with the kit.

Step One: Remove the rubber stopper from the test tube. Great! Just what she needed. A home science project for extra credit. *Step Two: Fill the dropper with urine up to the indicated line. Step Three: Add the urine to the test tube and mix with the powder in the tube, by gently shaking it from side to side. Step Four: Unwrap the color key and place the narrow end into the tube. You may read your results after five minutes.*

The next five minutes were among the longest Julie could imagine. She stared at the color key. Was the circle closest to the bottom going to turn pink? *No, please don't. Please don't change color.* She squatted down so she was eye level with the test, but most of the color key was blocked by the little paper stand that held the test tube.

She stood up and peered at her reflection in the mirror on the medicine cabinet. She didn't *look* any different. Brown eyes, strong, slightly upturned nose, full mouth. Maybe more tired looking than usual—but why wouldn't she be after what she'd been going through?

Or was it this other thing that was making her so exhausted? She made a face at herself in the mirror. She and Matt should have known better. No matter what the circumstances. Disgusted, she turned away and glanced at the second hand on her watch. Two minutes and a bit. Three minutes. She fixed her eye on the test tube and made another silent invocation. *Negative. Let it be negative.*

She sat down on the closed seat of the toilet. She and Matt, parents? No way. She was a freshman in college. And Matt— The chilling thought took hold of her: *Matt might not even—*

No! She couldn't let herself think that way. Matt had been doing too much of that himself.

Matt was going to live. And the test had to come out negative.

She picked up the instructions from the kit and studied the section called "Reading the Results." There was an illustration of a color key. Three circles ran down the key. A pink one, a white one, and at the bottom of the key, a circle with a tiny question mark inside it.

If you have performed this test correctly, the top circle will be pink, the instructions read. *The middle circle will be white. THE BOTTOM CIRCLE SHOWS YOUR RESULTS. If the bottom circle is white and matches the middle circle, your result is NEGATIVE. If your regular menstrual cycle has been delayed more than two weeks, you may wish to repeat this test in a few days. If the color of the bottom circle is pink and matches the color of the top circle, your result is POSITIVE. Consult your doctor immediately.*

"Immediately." As in "emergency." Julie looked at her watch again. Four and a half minutes. She was aware of every nerve in her body. Only thirty seconds until she knew. She watched the second hand sweep around her watch as she counted backward. Twenty-nine, twenty-eight . . . three, two, one. She closed her eyes for a moment, her pulse pumping through her body in panic. She took a deep breath, opened her eyes, and removed the color key from the test tube.

Her eyes went directly to the bottom circle. All she saw was pink. As pink a pink as she'd ever seen. Her breath caught in her throat. It had to be a mistake. Julie looked at the directions again, then back at the color key she held in her trembling hand. Pink. No mistaking it. Bright pink. Julie was pregnant.

Twenty-five

Julie found them at the second-floor study carrels. Both of them. Together. Dahlia and Nick were sitting where she and Nick used to look for each other back when they'd first met at the beginning of the year. Except instead of sitting side-by-side in two separate carrels, Dahlia and Nick had pulled two chairs up to one carrel and were bent over the same book, heads almost touching—her blond head and his sandy-brown one. Dahlia had called Julie the morning after her date with Nick, eager to replay every detail, but it was the first time Julie had seen her friends together, really together. It was a little strange. Nice, but strange.

"Hi," Julie said.

They both looked up. Happy embarrassment flashed across their faces. "Hey, Julie!" Dahlia said, with a silly grin.

Julie was glad for them—and they looked awfully cute together. Still, it was hard to feel more than a distant kind of reaction. Every part of Julie's being, her very soul, was focused inward, on what was happening inside her. A life was forming, a life that she and Matt had made even as his own life was in danger of being snuffed out.

What did it look like, right now? Was it any bigger than a seed? Would it grow into a boy or a girl? Deep in Julie's womb, created in a night of love, was the beginning of a human being. She brought her hands to her belly. It was really happening. It was a miracle. And it was terrifying.

Dahlia's dreamy grin melted into a frown of concern. "Julie? Are you feeling okay?"

"Stomachache?" Nick asked.

Julie let her hands fall away from her abdomen. She shook her head. "No. No, it's not that."

"Matt!" Nick said, his voice shot with worry.

"It's not Matt," Julie said quickly. *Well, it's partially Matt,* she thought. But it wasn't what Nick was afraid of. "He's all right and everything. At least, I think so." Julie tried to get a hold on herself. She took a few breaths. The girl at the carrel behind them had turned to shhh them. "Look, I'm really sorry to bother you guys, but . . . well, I really need to talk to Dahlia. Girl talk," Julie added, before Nick could look hurt.

"I think we were about ready for a study break anyway," Dahlia said. "Weren't we?" She looked up at Nick. *We.* In other circumstances, Julie might have suppressed the urge to giggle. Now she was just glad her friends were here for her.

"Yeah, sure. Meet you back here in a few, Dahlia?" Nick put his hand on Dahlia's arm. They leaned toward each other for a final kiss.

A few minutes later, Julie and Dahlia were seated cross-legged on the lawn of Central Bowl, outside the library. Julie picked at a blade of grass. She could feel Dahlia staring at her with a mixture of worry and curiosity. Julie looked up at her. "I'm pregnant," she said.

Dahlia let out a gasp. "Oh, my God!" Then, a moment later: "Is it . . ." Her sentence trailed off.

"Dahlia!" Julie protested.

"Well, I meant, of course it's Matt's," Dahlia backpedaled. "I didn't really think . . . Oh, you know. Wow, that's intense." She let out a low whistle.

Julie felt a tiny smile forming on her lips. She put a palm on her belly again. "Yeah. It *is* incredible. First comes love . . ."

"So was it—on purpose?" Dahlia wanted to know.

Julie's smile vanished. "With Matt in the hospital?" She shook her head. "He doesn't even know yet."

"You're going to tell him, aren't you?" Dahlia asked.

Julie sighed. "He's been so depressed. I'm really afraid."

"Maybe it will give him something to be happy about," Dahlia suggested. "I mean, it's a pretty amazing thing."

"Yeah, except that Matt's attitude being what it is these days, it might make him feel even worse. He'll just wonder if he's even going to be around to see it." Julie swallowed hard. There was a lump in her throat. "Maybe he won't."

Dahlia reached out and touched Julie's arm. "So, what are you going to do?"

Julie shrugged miserably. "I don't know. I guess if Matt's going to—if anything's going to happen to him, at least I'd have something left of him. But it might be too sad." She closed her eyes, the crisp sunshine painting an orange wash behind her eyelids. Then she opened them. Dahlia was watching her, full of concern. "I have no idea what to do."

"Julie, the baby's half his," Dahlia reminded her softly. "Don't you think he has a right to know?"

"Well, of course I'm going to tell him," Julie said. "Eventually. But I was thinking maybe I should wait until he's out of the hospital. I mean, he's in the middle of chemo now. I'm just not sure he can handle another thing—especially something so huge."

"Maybe it would be good for him," Dahlia said. "Give him something to think about besides his illness."

Julie considered this. "Maybe. But it's so scary. I mean, to be parents—me and Matt, a mother and father, in the middle of all of this."

"Julie, you told me Matt needed something to get him fighting again," Dahlia reasoned.

"He does." There was a moment of quiet. The sun was warm on Julie's face.

"Wow, imagine how cute a baby of yours and Matt's would be."

Julie wondered what it would look like. Would it have Matt's deep-set gray eyes? Her round face? Would it be an adventurer, like Matt? Inquisitive, like her?

"Tell him, Julie," Dahlia encouraged. "He can handle it. Nick keeps saying that if there's one thing Matt likes, it's a challenge."

"He used to, anyway." Julie sighed.

"Matt?"

The first thing Matt saw when he opened his eyes was Julie's face—big brown eyes, strong nose with its slight upward curve, full lips. As he took in more of the picture, he noticed she was more dressed up than when she usually came to visit. She wore her favorite Indian-print dress with her big silver hoop earrings. Her dark hair was shiny, lying in loose waves around her shoulders. What was the big occasion? Had she gotten decked out just to pay a visit to a place full of terminal cases?

"Were you sleeping? I didn't wake you, did I?" she asked.

"Huh? No. I was sort of half and half."

"Where's Danny?"

Matt looked over and saw that his bed was still freshly made from this morning. "Still not back yet, I guess. He was having a rough time in chemo this morning. Sometimes he doesn't respond too well. It happens."

"Oh. Poor guy," she said.

"He'll be okay, Julie," Matt said without emotion. He just couldn't bring himself to admit out loud how bad Danny's condition was getting. Somehow, Matt felt that thinking the worst about Danny was like getting in the way of his dreams and his plans for a future. Matt wasn't about to rob Danny of the life he wanted so badly. "He's okay," Matt repeated.

"I hope so," Julie said. "How about you? How was the treatment today?"

"Same. Awful. Painful," Matt muttered. "I

don't want to talk about it. You want to watch some tube?" he asked, gesturing at the screen that was now showing Bugs Bunny cartoons. "There's a great old gangster movie coming on in a little while. It's supposed to be—"

"Matt," Julie interrupted. "We have to talk." She suddenly had that seriously worried look on her face, the deep frown and the wrinkly nose, the one she got lately whenever she disapproved of his negative attitude, which was just about all the time, it seemed.

"If it's about me and my cancer, forget it. I don't want to talk about it, Julie."

Julie walked over, shut the TV off, then came back and sat down on his bed. Matt felt trapped. He could barely move, and she wasn't relenting. "It's not about your cancer. It's about us," she said, the weight of her words dropping like a lead weight. "All of us."

Matt felt suddenly on edge. "Us? All of us?" What did she mean, us? Was it time for her to bail out? Is that what she'd gotten all dressed up for? To tell him she was calling it quits? Had she spent enough time taking care of a cancer patient? "What about us?" he asked.

"Matt, this is really hard for me to say, especially under the circumstances." Julie was running her hand nervously through her hair. Her eyes didn't meet Matt's.

"Come on, Julie. Just tell me," he said,

readying himself for a fatal blow.

Julie took an audible breath. "I—I'm pregnant."

Matt heard the words, but they didn't seem to make sense. Pregnant? Not possible. Matt was sick with cancer. They hadn't made love since—

"We're going to have a baby, Matt," Julie said.

"But, Julie, I don't get it. We haven't made love in months."

"That's right, two-and-a-half months," she said. "Remember when you came home from the doctor's office with the bad news?"

Matt thought over that day, step by step. He'd ridden home on his motorcycle, promising himself he'd tell Julie right away, without making it too depressing. But it was impossible, because as soon as the words were out, they were both in tears, hugging each other with all their might. Matt remembered the rest, too. They'd made love. Right on the living-room floor. Passionately, as if their lives depended on it, immediately. *Immediately!* It was starting to sink in. "Oh, my God—"

They both looked at each other with guilty eyes. Matt felt a rush of emotions and fears filling his head.

He lay back and shut his eyes. It didn't make sense. A baby? Now? When he was struggling with cancer? But he might be dead in a few months. He barely had the will to live anymore. No, it couldn't happen like this. It wasn't supposed to happen like this.

"Matt?" Julie whispered softly.

He started to look away, but Julie grabbed for his hand and begged for his attention. "Don't shut me out, Matt. We have to talk about this," she said.

"I know, Julie. But, I mean, how am I supposed to feel? I'm lying here in the hospital. What are we supposed to do?" He couldn't keep the sharpness out of his voice.

Julie shrugged miserably. "I don't know. I don't even feel like we can deal with each other—let alone another human being."

Another human being. Matt felt a shiver of fear as he watched Julie brush away a trickle of tears.

"I've felt like you've been turning away from me," she said, sniffling. "Every time I try to be there for you—"

"I send you packing," Matt admitted. "Because I don't think you understand what I'm going through. It's like, in between your visits to the hospital I'm still here, slugging it out, and you're back home, living your own life."

"If you call what I've been doing living." Julie let out a long sigh. "I've been going out of my mind. Every night I get into bed and you're not next to me—healthy and happy—I feel totally empty. I wake up in the middle of the night crying."

"And then you come visit me and I act like I don't want you around."

Julie nodded.

Matt felt a sting of guilt and pain. Julie had been patient all along, through Matt's whole wretched illness. She *had* been there, through the worst of it. When he'd shut her out, she'd done all she could to let him know she was still with him. Even when Matt had humiliated her, lashing out in anger in front of Nick at the movies, or when Dahlia had loaned them money and he'd acted as if Julie had done something wrong. She'd stuck by him through it all. She deserved so much more than what he'd given her. "Jules, I'm sorry about the way I've treated you. Really," Matt said. He reached for her hand. "I wish I could explain."

"You don't have to, Matt. I think I know how frightened you've been. But you know what? You just called me Jules." Still holding his hand, she sat down on the edge of his bed. "You haven't called me that in a long time."

Matt pulled her closer. Julie laid her head down on his chest. "I'm frightened, Matt." As he kneaded his hand into her shoulder blades, her tears flowed heavily.

Matt couldn't hold back a wave of his own tears. He held on to her tightly, closing his eyes, feeling the fear that enveloped them.

Hand in hand, they pressed their faces up close to the glass wall, looking in at a room full of newborns. Julie scanned the nursery, feeling a jolt of joy and amazement at the tiny, wrinkle-faced things, tucked snugly into their bassinets. Each baby had a little bracelet on its wrist, and a card at the foot of each bassinet announced the baby's name, birthday, height, and weight.

Julie spotted Samantha, a tiny, pinkish-red baby girl with a single, blond, wispy curl on the top of her head, her eyes shut tight, sleeping peacefully. Julie felt the wonder of life in the day-old infant's existence.

Matt tapped her on the shoulder. "Did you see Andrew? He's smiling at us."

"Don't you just feel like sneaking in there and giving each one of them a big wet kiss?"

"Definitely." Julie felt Matt's hand pressing gently against her stomach.

"A little lower," she said. "Yeah. Right there." It felt wonderful to have Matt's hand on the place where their baby was growing.

"One day soon, this is going to be our own little Samantha—or Andrew," Matt whispered, sounding as amazed as Julie felt.

"Then you do want to be a father," Julie said, almost afraid to breathe until she heard the answer.

There was a long pause. "I want to. More than anything. I'm just afraid— Well, you know what? I'm not going to think like that anymore," Matt said. Julie heard something in his voice she hadn't heard in a while. It was the call of a challenge. "The will to live," Matt said. "That's what I've needed all along."

"And here it is, right before our eyes," Julie said. "Isn't being part of a family as much a will as you could possibly need?"

Matt nodded. "Yeah, I guess it is." He caressed her stomach again. "Wow. It just feels like you. Maybe a little fleshier." He knelt down and kissed her stomach.

With his tender kisses, Julie's questions were being answered. Matt wanted the baby as much as she did. They were going to be a family. Julie began to feel a giant wave washing away all the misery and fear of the past months. The dreams and thoughts of tomorrow were returning. "I love you, Matt."

"I love you, too, Julie." He gave her stomach another kiss. "And I love you, too— Hey, what are we going to name him, Jules?"

"You mean her." Matt looked up at her and they laughed. It felt so good to actually be laughing together! Finally, life felt good again.

Yet, even in their laughter, and the tender hug that followed, Julie knew that she and Matt still had a major battle with cancer ahead—and she knew that Matt was fully aware of it, too. But finally, after so many days of despair, they were both glad to feel alive again. Glad, and filled with new life.

Twenty-six

The class hour was almost up. Julie shut her journalism notebook and capped her pen.

"For next class, I'd like to focus on the idea that each newspaper has a particular personality. In preparation, I'd like an analysis of the same event covered three different ways in three different papers of your choosing," Professor Copeland concluded.

"How long?" someone called out from the back of the room.

Professor Copeland scowled. "As long as it takes." He shook his head. "Any other questions? Good. Oh, and Miss Miller, I'd like to see you after class for a moment."

Julie froze, halfway out of her seat. Her? Why? What had she done this time? Professor Copeland had been hard on her since day one of first semester, but she thought they'd been getting along better lately.

Across the aisle, John Graham shot Julie a questioning look. She raised her shoulders. "Good luck," he mouthed.

Julie put her notebook and pen into her bag and slung the bag over her shoulder. Her heart beating nervously, she approached Professor Copeland. Julie saw that all the pooper-scooper articles were in a pile on his desk—and hers was on top.

Professor Copeland waited until all the other students had filed out. Julie stood there, her pulse racing. "Very nice piece of work," he finally said, patting the pile of papers.

"It was?" Julie was so prepared for a problem that the praise took her by surprise.

"Balanced, informative, but amusing," he added.

He liked it. Mean Professor Copeland actually liked her article on dog poop. Julie allowed herself a small grin. "Thank you, sir."

"You're welcome, Julie. Bothersome assignment, I know. But journalists get assigned practically anything to write about," he said, a smile creeping across his face. A smile? Copeland? "Now, I'm also impressed that you got this little assignment in on time, despite your husband's illness."

Julie felt a jolt of surprise. "You know about

that?" Professor Copeland had always been so formal, so distant. Julie hadn't even known if her teacher knew she was married!

"Yes, and I think you handled yourself in a most professional way," he said. "How is your husband, Miss Miller?"

"Still fighting it. But his spirits are high. That's important," Julie said. She thought about the change in Matt's mood since he'd heard the news about the baby, and she felt a surge of happiness. Almost immediately, her hand went to her stomach.

"Indeed, that's good to hear." Professor Copeland said. "Now let me get to the point."

Julie felt her nervousness return. So Professor Copeland hadn't asked to see her in order to compliment her work, or ask about Matt. "Yes, sir?"

"Every year, Miss Miller, I am asked to recommend one student for a summer position at the Madison *Register*."

Julie felt her heart skip. A job on a real newspaper? Was Professor Copeland saying what she thought he was?

"I've been rather pleased with the progress you've made in my class," he said. "I think you could learn quite a lot working at the *Register*. Pardon the pun, but your piece on the pooper-scooper law certainly would have been more interesting than the excrement they printed," he added bitingly.

Julie's laughter was tinged with amazement. "You mean, you're offering me a job, sir?"

"Well, no, I'm not in a position to offer you the job," he said. "But I'd like to recommend you. Now, you understand, of course, that some of the reporting you'd do might not even be as interesting as this little assignment." He touched the pile of papers again.

"Actually, sir, I kind of liked doing the interviewing for that article—meeting the people of Madison and talking to them."

Professor Copeland nodded seriously. "I see I'm recommending the right person."

"I was wondering what I'd do here for work this summer." *Especially with the baby coming,* she thought to herself.

"You understand I'm recommending you on merit, not on need."

Oh. Did that mean the job on the *Register* was volunteer? Julie felt a sting of disappointment. If that was the case, then she couldn't afford to take it. They still had to pay back Dahlia, and then there was the student loan, more medical bills, and soon there would be another mouth to feed. Julie was suddenly consumed by a feeling of enormous responsibility.

"There is, of course, a salary," he said.

Julie breathed a quiet sigh of relief.

"But I want to stress again, Miss Miller, that I've chosen you because I think you show a lot of promise. It was not a decision based on need."

"Yes, sir." So much praise coming from Professor Copeland, Julie could hardly believe it. "Thank you, sir."

"You're welcome," he said. "Then I take it you're interested?"

Writing news stories instead of serving overcooked vegetables? Doing what she'd always dreamed she'd someday do? "Absolutely!" Julie said.

"Good. I thought you might be, Miss—Ms. Miller."

The intensive-care room was exactly as Matt remembered it. Lots of nurses, lots of machines beeping and blinking, and lots of people in pain. The only difference was that, tonight, Matt was there not as a patient, but as a visitor. He sat in a chair at Danny's bedside, unable to take his eyes off his little friend. Matt held a stack of baseball cards in his hand. He'd brought them from their room, hoping Danny would be awake to see them.

Lying there, eyes closed to the world, Danny looked strangely peaceful. Silent and completely still—a tiny child amid tons of high-tech metal machinery, I.V. bags, and plastic tubing. Matt prayed for him to open his eyes and join the world again. But Danny had gone into a coma. He was now fighting what could be his final battle.

A nurse, her face hidden by a green mask, came by to check his vital signs. She'd been doing it every fifteen minutes or so for the past twelve hours. Danny lay there, oblivious to it all. Alive, but just barely. If not for the respirator that forced air into his lungs, it would have been over already. As the nurse scribbled numbers onto her clipboard, she caught Matt's eye and sadly shook her head. "Not even a miracle," she said.

About an hour ago, he'd heard another nurse say that Danny's parents were on their way. Matt swallowed hard, knowing that this could very well be the last long trip they'd have to make from their home over two hours away. He'd met Danny's parents only once, but he knew how much Danny meant to them. They'd spent the past few years of Danny's life shuttling him around the country to different cancer specialists. Soon their struggle would be over.

What about the Cubs? Matt thought. He'd shown Danny how to throw a curve. A real curveball. The little boy's hopes and dreams had become Matt's, too. He'd come to believe in them.

If ever there had been a fighter, it was Danny. He had more spirit in him than the rest of the patients in the ward times ten. And now?

Matt blew out a heavy breath of frustration. Danny deserved to live more than anybody. *So, why this? Why Danny and not me?* he thought, almost guiltily. But he stopped himself from taking that one any further. *Not me!* he swore.

Looking at Danny now, so little life left, he could feel the emptiness already. But there were so many reasons for Matt to keep fighting. His life was still so full. Julie meant the world to him. And now there was a baby on its way. The adventure of a lifetime lay ahead of him. He had a family who needed him. And Danny. Matt had to survive for Danny, too. Danny would want him to keep up the fight.

He felt he should say good-bye. Say something, anyway. But now, it seemed as though it was too late. Chances were that Danny would never wake up again.

"Hey, Danny. Can you hear me, buddy?" Matt spoke out loud. No movement, nothing. "It's okay, stay still. You need your rest. Hey, did I tell you the big news? About Julie and me? Yep, you guessed it. We're going to have a baby. Incredible, huh? Julie keeps telling me it's going to be a girl, but I'm sure it'll be a boy. Hey, you won't mind if I teach him how to throw a few pitches, will you?"

Matt didn't try to hold back the tears. He sat there, watching Danny, tasting the salt as it trickled down his face. "Hey, you never did finish that book on the history of the World Series. I saw you were just getting up to '56.

Wow, what a year that was! You ever hear about Don Larsen? He was a pitcher, like you, Danny. His curveball was okay, not great. Actually, this guy Larsen, he wasn't much different from you or me. He was sort of a regular guy. But in the 1956 World Series he had his day. Boy, did he ever! Probably the greatest day anybody ever had in baseball. He pitched to twenty-seven guys and mowed 'em all down. Not a single hit, not a single base runner. Larsen pitched the only perfect game in World Series history. It must have been something, Danny, because my dad used to tell me about it as if it was a greater accomplishment than landing on the moon."

Matt wondered if anything was getting through. For a second it looked almost as if Danny was smiling. Maybe he'd heard. "A regular guy, Danny, that's what he was, just a regular guy like you or me. But he had his day."

Matt paused. He looked down and realized he still had the baseball cards in his hand. He looked once more at Danny. His face was childlike, calm. Matt took the cards and slipped them under the covers, placing them in Danny's hand. "To you and me, Danny. May we both have our day."

Twenty-seven

Julie peeked her head around the door of Matt's hospital room. He was staring off in the direction of Danny's empty bed, a glazed expression on his face. "Hey!" she said softly.

Matt turned. "Julie. Hi." He managed a little smile.

Julie sat down on the edge of his bed and leaned toward him, until her lips touched his. Matt kissed her softly, a quick, feather-light kiss. Then his arms went around her and he kissed her again, longer, his lips moist and searching. Julie was surprised at the strength with which he held her. "Mmm. That's the medicine," he murmured, kissing her again. "It's lonely around here."

As they separated, Julie looked over at Danny's side, too. The wall above his bed looked bare without the Cubs pennant. Ten years and his life was over. Even Mary Beth's short life had been longer than that.

"Nurse Rodriguez says they're going to put someone else in here this evening," Matt said, following Julie's gaze. "Gone. That's it. Yesterday he was here, and now—" He gave a sharp, short laugh. "I remember Danny telling me how there was some guy here before me. I asked what happened to him. He just kind of shrugged and went on to another subject. Someone before me, and before him, and after him . . ."

Julie's body went tight. The last thing Matt needed was another reason to get depressed—so depressed that he didn't have the will to fight.

"Danny was a great kid," Matt went on. "But I don't have to be one of the unlucky ones. I mean, I've got the most important reason in the world to get better. Two of them." He reached out and put his hand on Julie's stomach. "How's the baby?"

Julie felt an assuring wave of happiness. "The baby's going to be beautiful. I'm seeing my doctor the day after tomorrow. As soon as he says everything's fine, I want to tell our parents, okay?"

"Definitely. It'll be nice to maybe bring them a little closer over some *good* news for a change." Matt laughed and shook his head. "Grandpa Fast Lane. Yes, junior, your old grandfather really was a famous race-car driver, once upon a time!" Despite Matt's gaunt but swollen face, despite the patches of stubble on his bald scalp, he looked like the old Matt. His deep-set gray eyes sparkled, and a hint of challenge played at his full lips. Dahlia was right. Matt liked to see what he could take on. And he liked to win—from high mountains to Club Night to licking the disease inside him.

"And how's my other baby?" he asked.

"She's fine, too. I'm still nauseated in the morning, but knowing why, I don't mind so much," Julie said. "Oh, and hey—you won't believe this—Copeland actually wants to recommend me for a summer job at the *Register*."

"Professor Copeland? Really? A real job?"

Julie nodded. "Yeah. He actually loved the article, so he's going to send it and some of my other stuff to the *Register* with his recommendation. I mean, it's the kind of thing I'd do just for the experience, but if they hire me, I'll get paid and everything!"

"Wow! And one day, when you're a famous journalist and someone asks you what launched your career, you'll have to tell them it was a mound of dog—"

"Matt!" Julie cut him off, laughing. "Anyway, I don't have the job yet. But he only recommends one student, so there's a really good chance."

"I know you'll get it," Matt said. "We're going to have to get you some professional-looking maternity clothes."

Julie grinned. "Taken care of already. I think Dahlia intends to ship me every piece of maternity clothing in her father's store."

"Is she waiting downstairs?" Matt asked.

Julie nodded. "With Nick. It's like they have to make up for all the time they didn't like each other, or something. She even let him drive the BMW here."

"Ah, new love," Matt joked.

Julie laughed. "They said they'd give us a little while alone and then come up to say hi. If they can separate their mouths for a— Oh, hi, Dr. Zinn!" she finished, as the young, bearded doctor came into the room, clipboard in hand.

Matt gave him a little wave. "Hi. See? Still in bed, still taking care of myself," he announced with a smile.

"Hi, everyone," Dr. Zinn said. He grinned as he crossed the room to the side of Matt's bed. He held out the clipboard. "I wanted you to see this, Matt. You, too, Julie."

Matt took the clipboard and Julie peered over his shoulder. The top page was printed with a column of long, Greek-looking words that Julie couldn't even pronounce, let alone understand: *Erythrocytes, leukocytes, platelets, mytosis.* . . . Next to them, a confusion of numbers and letters had been written in by hand. Julie had no idea what any of it meant.

She looked at Matt. He shrugged his shoulders and raised an eyebrow. "Looks very official," he said to Dr. Zinn. "Wanna translate?"

"Quite simply, it means your cancer is now in remission," he announced with a broad smile.

For a long moment, Julie and Matt were completely silent. Julie had heard the doctor's words, but they still hadn't registered. She reached for the clipboard and started scanning the chart again. Where did it say Matt was better?

"Trust me, Julie," Dr. Zinn said. "Matt's going to be fine."

A giant smile broke out over Matt's face. "Yes!" he shouted, punching a victory fist in the air. "I knew it!"

Julie felt her heart flutter. She was swept by a heady, dizzying joy. She clapped her hands like a little kid. Matt was going to be fine! She felt suddenly light, the worry and fear of the past months lifted.

Matt straightened up. "Then I'm outta here? I can go home?" His voice was wild with anticipation.

"Whoa, not so fast. I'm afraid you're still going to need to do chemo—"

Julie watched a jolt of panic wash over Matt's face.

"—for another two months maximum. Maximum," Dr. Zinn repeated. "That's how long it's going to take to fully wipe out the cancer."

"Two more months. And then I'm cured. I can live with that," Matt said. Julie watched the smile returning to his face. "Jules, did you hear? Two months and I'm all better!"

Julie wiped away a joyous tear. "Thank you, Dr. Zinn," she said. "I can't tell you how great I feel right now."

"I think I have an idea," he said. "It's people like you two who remind me why I wouldn't want any other job."

Matt extended his hand to the doctor. "You're the best," he said. "I couldn't have gone the distance without you. Thank you so much."

Two months, thought Julie. This was early April. May, June. By June it would be over. She'd just be finishing her first year of college. She'd be starting to show by then. Maybe she'd even be able to feel the baby moving inside her. She might have her first professional job. And she and Matt would have the entire summer ahead of them. The summer, and then a family, and a whole life together!

As soon as Dr. Zinn left the room, Julie was in Matt's arms. They looked into each other's eyes and no words were necessary. He cupped her face in his hands and kissed her eyelids. She breathed in his scent, feeling the warmth of his skin next to hers. They stayed like that for a moment, as if to capture the feeling.

Their mouths met. Their kiss was tender and slow, as if they had all the time in the world.

Don't miss Till Death Do Us Part,
the next book in this dramatic series

Julie left the Madison, Ohio, campus in Dahlia's little red convertible, top down, the September wind blowing her hair out behind her. Second gear. Clutch. Third gear. Release clutch. She was doing just fine. Now if Matt would only get his bike sold, she'd be all ready to drive their very own car.

Julie smiled as she cruised toward the highway. The landscape stretched out flat as far as the eye could see, but the trees were tipped with the first colors of fall, and the sky was huge overhead, a pale blue with lots of fluffy clouds.

She sang along with the music blaring out of the speakers. The speed and the wind and the music made her feel extra alive and free. She pressed down a little harder on the accelerator. The seat belt tight over her pregnant belly, she knew that she didn't have too many more weeks of this kind of freedom. There would be other pleasures. But not this feeling. Not for a long time again.

Julie pulled onto the four-lane highway that led out to the Madison-Shelton mall. Shift, fourth gear. She pulled into the left lane to pass the slow-moving flatbed truck in front of her, loaded with hay. Then back into the right lane. Up ahead, the highway curved sharply.

Slow down, Julie told herself. *Precious cargo on*

board. She put one hand on her stomach as she pressed the brake with her right foot. For a brief second, she heard a shrill squeak. Then the squeak stopped and the brake pedal collapsed to the floor of the car under her foot. The car didn't slow down.

Julie felt her body tighten with fear. But Dahlia had said not to worry about the squeak. She pushed down on the brake again. Nothing. It was like it wasn't connected to anything. The car was sailing full speed toward the curve in the road. Julie pumped the brake pedal faster, harder. The turn was right under her. She yanked the steering wheel to the right, clutching onto it and praying that the car would hold the road.

But as she steered around the turn, she came right up on a beat-up blue hatchback, moving too slowly in the right lane. She slammed her hand on the horn, but she was going so much faster than the car in front of her. She jerked the steering wheel back to the left to avoid smashing into the other car. The car lurched with the abrupt movement. The tires squealed. She was going into a skid.

Terror rose in Julie's chest. The car was sliding, slipping. The metal lane divider loomed up right in front of her eyes. *"No!"*

The scream wrenched from her throat met the sickening sound of shattering metal and glass. Julie pressed her hands over the baby. *Just like Mary Beth. Just like my sister. We're going to end up the same way. My baby and me. We're going to die.* It was the last thought she had.